The Streets Divine

Book I

Richanda Bynum

Copyright

The Streets Divine Book I

Copyright © 2022 by Richanda J. Bynum

For information contact:
Richanda Bynum
richanda.bynum.author@gmail.com

Library of Congress Control Number: 2022900362
ISBN- 13 978-1-957522-00-2
ISBN- 10 1-9757552-00-X

10 9 8 7 6 5 4 3 2 1

To my loving husband,
thank you for always
supporting me.
With you beside me, I know
can accomplish anything.

The Streets Divine

The Group

"Babe, can you hurry the fuck up? We're running late, and you got us down here waiting," I shout up the stairs at my loving husband.

"I'm coming. Calm yo ass down," Woo says, gliding down the stairs as if time doesn't matter. This man has the world in his palms, and he knows it.

My husband, Roland "Woo" Carver, can never be on time for anything. He has a lot of nerve. He's the one that kept reminding me about the meeting today. So I stand here asking myself, why the fuck am I dressed to the gods waiting at the bottom of the stairs? Woo is doing this shit on purpose. He knows good in damn well what it means for us to show up late to this fucking meeting.

"Fix yo face, or we not going any damn where," Woo says, kissing my lips.

I can't help the smile that spreads on my face. I lift my hand, caressing his beard as he pulls me closer. Damn, why does he have to be so fucking fine? Looking into my eye's knowing what I'm thinking, he smiles back at me. Why? Woo, don't do this. We have shit to do, and if you smile at me like this, we not going anywhere. I throw my arms around his shoulders, fuck it! He can take me upstairs right now.

"I thought I told you to fix yo face," Woo says, closing in on my lips once more.

As if an alarm went off in her head, Bobby comes running down the stairs, interrupting the moment my husband and I were having.

Alright, pause....

Before I go any further, I guess I should introduce myself and my family. I am Divine Carver, Queen of everything and loser of nothing. The handsome chocolate drop holding me in his arms right now is Roland, my husband of 8 years, but we call him Woo. On the couch over there minding his business looking down at his phone, that's Million, also known as "Milli," our adopted son. He just turned 18. Milli stays with me when he's not in school. I guess you could say he's a bodyguard of sorts. Where I go, he goes. I trust him with my life.

The beautiful woman walking down the stairs dressed in men's clothes, that's Roberta; we call her Bobby. She's Woo's right-hand man and fuck buddy. Yes, you read that right, fuck buddy. I must give it to her; she gets shit done, and as long as she knows her place, I could care less. Following her is the oriental beauty, Asia. She's another one that follows the scent of my husband's dick. These two are some pieces of work, but I guess I can get to that a little later. Right now, we need to get to this meeting.

Alright, play....

Pulling away from Woo, I can't help but roll my eyes.

"Let's go," I say, walking out of the door.

We all walk out of the house. Milli opens the car door for me. I get in and take a deep breath. I should be used to it, but I hate these fucking meetings. The Group is a meeting we must attend monthly. Fortunately, or unfortunately, all these years of committing crimes have paid off for me and Woo for good. Our organization became big enough to be offered a seat with The Group, or of course, we could have gone to war with every criminal on this side of the globe.

"Bobby, no trigger-happy shit today. I need for you to relax until I say the word." Bobby nods her head. I'm serious; this hoe is ready to kill anybody anywhere. "Asia, how about you and Bobby stay on Emilio? He's stupid, so he probably won't notice the two of you. I'm sure he's pissed about Milli taking care of his cousin."

I look at Woo, wondering if he has anything he'd like to add. He doesn't look up from his phone, but I know he feels my eyes on him.

"Divine, you got it. As always, let's make it out alive," Woo says.

I swear I have five kids. I look back at Milli; he has his headphones in, bobbing his head to his music. I smile at him; he nods at me, acknowledging that he knows to relax when we get in this building. Bobby pulls into the parking lot where you see nothing but exotic cars, fucking showoffs. Our bulletproof Suburban looks so bulky and out of place, but I'll take it over any of these fancy cars any day. Getting out of the car, Woo grabs my hand, pulling me next to him so we can walk side by side. Bobby and Asia lead the way into the building while Milli is on our tail. We're late, fuck!

Walking into the room that holds half the world's problems, all eyes are on us. Keeping my head held high, I walk in, swaying my hips. The floor is a runway, and I am the main model. Making it over to my seat, Woo pulls my chair out for me. I look at him giving him a smile; as usual, he has an expressionless face. This is how we are; I always have a beaming smile on my face with his holding a scowl. I like us this way; we're perfect for each other. I glance around the table, hoping this meeting goes off without a hitch.

"Woo, Divine, it's nice of you guys to finally join us," the head of The Group, Gavriil Ivanov, says, smirking.

Ignoring him, I glance over at Bobby; I raise my eyebrows quickly, giving her and Asia the signal to move. They discreetly make their way over to the other side of the room where trouble is. Milli stands behind Woo and me, watching the room, sure to see what we can't. Once things are in order on my side, I give Gavriil's sexy ass my attention.

"Time lost us," I say, smiling.

Smirking, "let us continue," Gavriil says, looking over at Emilio, "Emilio, as you were saying."

Emilio glares at me as he begins to speak.

"If we are supposed to make money without shedding blood, how is it that these motherfuckers," he holds his greasy, disgusting hand out, gesturing towards Woo and me, "who came in late disrespecting us all, think they can get away with killing one of my family?" I place my hand on my chest as if I'm shocked.

Guess we walked into a tension-filled room. I feel Woo's hand creep up my thigh, causing me to smile. Why does he want to play right now? This fool takes nothing seriously. Can't he see that Emilio is distressed about his family? This thought causes me to giggle a bit. I could care less about Emilio or his fucking family.

Gavriil looks over at me with narrowed eyes.

"Divine," I love the way my name rolls off his fucking tongue, "are Emilio's words true?"

I roll my eyes; Gavriil knows the answer yet as always, he must play this annoying diplomatic role. Fuck is he asking dumb questions for?

"Yes, what Emilio says is true." The whole room becomes quiet as I speak. "A bullet was put in his head on my order," I say the last part as I look at Emilio.

I want him to give a reason to jump stupid, fuck him! Just like I knew he would, Emilio jumps up from his seat. Stupid emotional fuck. His anger means nothing to me; however, the gun pinned to his skull right now lets me know that Bobby didn't like his sudden movements. If he was smarter, he would have seen her coming, but like his late cousin, he's a damn fool. One of Emilio's men has his gun out as well, pointed right at Bobby's head. No worries, Asia has her blade pressed right up against his dick.

"Try it, pretty boy, I dare you," Asia warns through gritted teeth. Then she plants a soft kiss on his cheek.

"Divine," Gavriil calls out, "you know this is a kill-free zone. We do not kill at a Group meeting. This is my one and only rule."

"The sooner Emilio takes his seat, the sooner we can get back to the meeting," I say, admiring my wedding ring.

"Bitch," Emilio spits out.

"Sit yo bitch ass down," Woo says.

I knew it was only a matter of time before Woo took over.

"Javi been harassing my little niggas for months. We tried that diplomatic shit; we came to you. Or did yo greasy ass forget? You chose not to sit his ass down, so we did it for you."

I smile, proud. Woo only speaks when necessary or when I am being disrespected. If Emilio wants to make it out alive, he better shut the fuck up. Once Woo starts, he doesn't quit. We are an unbreakable team, and every man in this room knows this. We back down for no one. If Emilio wants this to be his last day, I will gladly help him with his exit.

Emilio, finally understanding his position, takes his seat. Bobby puts her gun away. Backing away from him, she stands behind him. I look at Emilio as he glares at me; I know this isn't over.

"As always, you guys make the meeting more entertaining," Gavriil says, chuckling to himself.

Fuck! he is so damn sexy. I keep my eyes from looking at him; I need to focus.

"We did our part; we took it to Javi's leader. That's the shit you preach, right, Gavriil? That's the point of this Group shit, right? We followed protocol. Now let's continue this fucking meeting; we all got shit to do."

Every time Woo speaks, he commands the room, no one interrupts, and no one responds. Most of the men in this room have already had a piece of what Woo and I are capable of, most except Gavriil. I hate to admit it, but he is much more powerful than us. He has his family ties. All Woo and I have is each other. We are more than enough. If we ever have to take it there with Gavriil, I know we would win.

We continue with the meeting; Emilio glares at me the whole time. While ignoring him, I notice Gavriil glaring at

Woo every now and then. They hate each other, two alpha males in one room. I could list many reasons for their hatred. I mean, when Gavriil first approached Woo and me to join The Group, Woo refused. He was ready to go to war with every and anybody; that's how we survived this life in the first place. Me being the more rational one, I thought it through. It didn't sound like a bad idea. Being a part of The Group has helped us in ways we never dreamed of. It gave us connections we didn't know we were ready for. We were able to take our already growing empire to the next level. So, there's that. Then there's the fact that I'm fucking Gavriil, occasionally.

First Friend

I am not a hoe; alright, fine, maybe I am. Whatever, things weren't always like this between Woo and me. When we were younger and much poorer, things were better and different. Woo and I met when I was twelve, and he was fourteen. Our mothers were what one would call crack hoes. Somehow some way, they always ended up at the crack house together, leaving Woo and me to fend for ourselves. By the time we met, we'd already been through so much. I'd seen him and his mom around, but because my mother didn't think I could take care of myself, she kept me locked in our raggedy apartment. It wasn't until I was twelve that she let me out.

Woo being someone going through the same things as me made me feel like he understood me. To get my mind off how horrible my life was, Woo would always take me to the park and push me on the swings. Even then, he didn't talk much; I usually did the talking. Every now and then, I'd hear a grunt or an 'aight', letting me know that he was at least pretending to listen. When he did speak, it was always about kings and queens. He liked to talk about empires. Woo loved ancient Rome. Gladiator was one of his favorite movies, I hadn't seen it at the time, so I could only take his word for how good it was.

The kids in the neighborhood would talk shit about us and our appearance, but never around Woo. Even when we were younger, he had that don't fuck with me face. They'd do that hateful shit when I was by myself, as I was weak back then, soft. They would throw rocks and shit, causing me to cry like a little baby bitch. Somehow some way, Woo would always show up, saving me and beating those kids' ass.

Woo became everything, the first person I ever had in my corner. Whenever my mother would drag me to that crack house with her, forcing me to sit in the front yard, I was happy. I knew Woo and his mother would eventually walk around the corner.

Woo was older and bigger, so he didn't have to follow his mother around as I did. Woo felt he needed to protect her, so he was always one step behind her, well, when she allowed him to be. This always made me envious of him. All the shit she'd made him survive, and he still loved her. I, on the other hand, hated Keisha, my mother. Woo and I became 'crack baby friends,' or a least that's what the other kids called us. Even when I think about my past now, I don't mind the name. It was a name I shared with Woo.

Realizing that we'd starve if we didn't get food for ourselves, I came up with this wonderful plan to get us money for food. It was an easy plan in my young, naïve mind. The thought came naturally to me; all I had to do was hoe, sell myself like I watched my mother do daily. I remember feeling happy that I'd come up with a plan to get us some money. I remember going to Woo with a smile on my face.

"Woo," I said, running up to him. He was sitting on the curb.

"Divine," he said, looking at the ground.

Whenever I called out to him, he never stopped what he was doing, but he would always acknowledge me.

"I know a way we can make some money." He looked up at me, curious. "I could just turn some tricks, and you can look out for me."

I must admit, I wasn't a smart child. Like everyone around me, I was a product of my environment. I remember the look on his face; it was a look he only made when he was fighting the other kids for me. He looked around quickly as if making sure no one had heard what I had just said. Woo grabbed me by my arm and pulled me down the street till we got to an alley.

"Why you dragging me? Woo, what's wrong?" I whined.

At the time, I didn't understand his anger.

"You so fucking stupid." I never heard his voice this deep, this loud. "You wanna be a hoe, just like yo momma, just like mine? And you want me to be yo fucking pimp?"

The next thing I knew, my body had hit the ground. Woo slapped the shit out of me. This was the first time in my life that someone I loved hurt me. I knew long before I could understand that I didn't care for my momma, and she didn't care for me. But Woo was someone that I thought the world of. I began sobbing uncontrollably; he needed to calm down. Why was he so mad?

"Shut the fuck up," Woo yelled at me. "This is how hoes get treated. This is how a pimp takes care of his hoe. Is this how you wanna be out here living?" he asked.

Lifting my head up, I looked at him through tear-filled eyes. I held my cheek tightly. Woo was looking down at me, angry and pissed. His whole body was shaking, and his eyes were watering. I hurt him, and at the time, I didn't understand how. I only wanted to help, figure out a way for us to eat.

"Divine, answer me, you wanna be a hoe?"

Standing to my feet, "No, Woo, I'm sorry. Please don't be mad at me," I pled. Woo was all I had in the world. My young heart couldn't take him hating me. "Woo, I'm sorry."

Grabbing the back of my head, he pulled me to his chest.

"Don't ever say no shit like that again." He sighed, "I won't say sorry. I needed to make sure you understood. I'll think of something, we gone eat. But we won't be like them."

I nodded my head against his chest; I felt relief that he wasn't mad at me, that he was holding me in his arms. Woo was my everything.

With me not tricking and Woo not being my pimp, we had to find another way to survive. Woo told me I could no longer be a "fucking crybaby ass punk" if I was going to be his partner. He said that I couldn't be a baby anymore. I had to man up because we had real shit to do. Woo and I became stick-up kids. We would steal any and everything. We mostly stole from pimps and drug dealers; at that time, those were the only people we knew who had money. And we were good at it.

Sometimes I got to act; I would be the young honey looking for a date or the damsel crying in the street waiting to be turned out. Who knew there were so many perverts out there preying on a twelve-year-old girl? No matter when or where, Woo was always in the shadows waiting to bust the poor bastard that fell for my trap in the head with the butt of the gun; he'd bought off a crack head.

By the time I was thirteen and Woo fifteen, we were experts at stealing. We had complete trust in each other. Woo was right; I couldn't be a crybaby anymore. We found an abandoned building and started living in it, and we kept all our stuff in it. We couldn't take anything home. I'm sure Woo would have killed my mom and his if they'd stolen the shit, being that we risked our lives for. We were putting our lives on the line every day, and to us, it was worth it. Our appearances started to change as well. We could buy clothes and food, and we were looking like all the other kids, no more dirt, no more grime.

While surviving and taking things one day at a time, I got to thinking.

"Woo," I said, looking out of the window of the abandoned building we were squatting in.

"Divine," he said flatly.

"When was the last time you seen yo mom?" I looked over at him, and he looked up from counting the money we'd stolen earlier in the day.

"Damn," he said, putting the money down in a shoe box. I watched as he ran his hands through his rough and coarse hair. "It's been like a month."

"Right. Usually, if I go two days without checking on my mom, she'd start walking the streets screaming my name, 'Divine, where's Mommas Divine pussy?'" I mocked.

Woo laughed because he knew I was right. I had a bad feeling.

"Let's go to they spot and see for ourselves," he said, standing while putting his gun in his pants and handing me mine.

Walking up the same block we used to roam around a year ago, things seemed different. Or maybe we were different; people stared at us, kids pointed at us. I was unfazed. Woo and I made it a point to do all our bullshit on the other side of town. So, people that wanted to find us wouldn't be able to so easily. Walking up to the neighborhood crack house, Woo kicked the door in. I said nothing and just followed him quietly.

Walking around the dirty house, some crackheads we knew, some we didn't. They were of no help because they were all nodding off into Lala land. Angry, Woo stomped out of the house; I followed, already knowing where he was headed. He walked up the street to a group of dope boys in the middle of a dice game. He was looking for the one our mothers loved to cop crack from.

"Doug, you seen Raven?" Woo asked in his usual quiet voice.

I don't know if Doug was ignoring him, but he didn't even turn around to acknowledge us. Getting impatient, I walked up, tapping Doug on the shoulder.

Doug turned around with an attitude, "fuck yall little niggas want?"

"Woo asked you if you seen Raven," I said, not backing down.

"Oh shit, yall ain't heard." He looked back at his boys, then back to us, "you little mothafuckas been hitting the streets so hard that yall ain't know both yall mommas overdosed." Doug said this as if it wasn't something that could shake our world.

"Yo, why you say it to them like that?" one of the guys standing with him said.

"Overdosed," I heard Woo say from behind me.

"Yeah, they were at the spot when that shit happened. Yall all around the world, sticking people up and didn't even know. The whole hood knows what yall little asses been up to. Just don't bring that fuck shit around..." Before Doug could even finish his sentence, Woo was at him.

I didn't know why, nor did I care. I pulled my gun and pointed it at the group of dudes, daring them to interfere. For Woo, I would kill all of them.

"Damn Doug, you out here getting yo ass beat by a fucking kid," a bystander shouted, laughing.

Once Woo had enough, he stood looking down at Doug and kicked him. "Fuck what the hood knows!" he said loud enough for the dope boys and me to hear.

"Was that necessary? You got it, little Woo, you got it," one of the dudes said. "Tell shorty to put that piece down."

"Naw fuck that. We don't know yall, so we don't trust yall. Now back the fuck up." Woo said.

He then looked at me as if asking me a question. I knew what he was asking, so I nodded, not caring. I had my piece on them already, so we proceeded to rob them.

"Yall know we gone see yall, right?" some dude said.

"So," I said, pulling the trigger. I was aiming at his leg but shot him in the ass. He began screaming out in pain.

Woo grabbed my arm, and we started running away, I heard gunshots going off behind us, but I refused to look back. At this moment, where any of those bullets could have hit me, I was looking at Woo as we ran for our lives. If I was going to die, I wanted him to be the last thing I saw, to be young again.

Stopping to check ourselves and catch our breaths, I began laughing. I looked up at Woo, and he had tears in his eyes. He loved Raven; I had no feelings towards Kiesha. Kiesha never did anything for me; she just birthed me into this world and promised to sell my pussy to the highest bidder when it was ripe. I did feel a bit lonely though. Even if she was trash, she was still the only family I had.

"We gotta go to Bo's," Woo said, looking over my head. It was like he couldn't see me.

"For what?" I asked, curious. Bo was Raven's old pimp.

"I gotta get something."

"Alright, lead the way."

Arriving at the old apartment building that we both once called home, we ran up the flights of stairs, making it to the top floor. Woo began banging on the door with the number twelve on it. I looked down the hall at the door that had the number ten on it, which was once my prison. Before Keisha thought I was old enough to take care of myself, she'd leave me in there hungry for days. Then she'd show up with a cold happy meal and tell me to eat. A small beat-up woman that I'd never seen before answered the door. Woo, not caring about knocking her over, burst through the door.

"No, you can't come in here. Bo's not here. He's going to be mad at me again," she cried out.

Ignoring her, I walked into the apartment. I looked in the kitchen and saw a little boy tucked away in the corner. If she was so scared of Bo, she shouldn't have opened the door in the first place. Or at least that's what he was going to say when he beat her ass. Woo came from the back of the apartment with a backpack on. He grabbed my hand, pulling me out of the door; my feet wouldn't move. Without saying anything, I pointed to the kitchen corner at the little boy. Woo looked in the direction I was pointing to.

"Who the fuck is that, and why is he in here?" I heard Woo shout. Remembering the horror stories Woo told me about his time in this house with his mother's pimp, I walked over to the little boy.

The small beat-up woman got on her knees in front of Woo, "please take him, just take him, get him away from here. Get him away from Bo."

I looked back at the woman, surprised. She was begging us to take her son; Bo would surely kill her ass for this. The woman looked at me as if reading my mind.

"He's going to kill me anyway once he sees all his money gone," she said in a whisper.

I looked at Woo, making eye contact. This fool brought us here to rob a psycho. Woo walked over to me, handing me the backpack. He grabbed the little boy putting him on his back. The little boy didn't even put up a fight.

"We gotta go, and we ain't coming back," Woo said, looking me in the eyes.

"Alright," is all I said before I followed him out of the door.

That night we went back across town to our abandoned building. We fed ourselves and the little boy then we all cuddled up together on the air mattress to keep warm.

"This the last time we sleeping like this," Woo said from behind me in my ear.

I pulled the little boy closer to me; I needed to keep him warm.

"What you mean?" I asked, sleepy.

"From now on, we sleeping in beds. Fuck this hard life shit," Woo held me tighter.

"Woo."

"Divine."

"What did we just do?" I said, finally asking what I'd been longing to know since we left the hoe house.

"On her normal days, Raven always told me the code to Bo's safe. She said she saw him put it in one night. He thought she was too high to remember it or something, I guess. She was too scared to do it, but she told me if I ever needed to get away from here to make sure I make that nigga fund my trip."

I took a deep breath before my next question. Sure, I was young and dumb, but I knew hurt when I saw it.

"Are you ok, Woo?"

Woo tucked his head into my neck, "I'll never be ok Divine, and neither will you." Hearing this made me sad a bit. "Raven was so many things, but I still loved her. We alone for real now, Divine. All we got is each other."

I closed my eyes. Even if Raven was like Keisha, I could see why Woo loved her. At least he had fond memories of her, unlike me with Keisha.

Forever Loyal

I remember waking up to Woo gone with the backpack the next morning, leaving just the kid and me. The little boy stared at me as I stared at him.

"What's your name?" I asked.

He shook his head.

"Ok, how old are you?" I asked this time with a smile on my face.

It took him a moment, but he held his hand up, displaying all five of his fingers.

"Oh wow, you're five years old."

He nodded his head up and down.

"So, five-year-old boy, do you have a name?"

He shook his head. I began getting excited. I stood up and began pacing around in a circle. While I was in the middle of thinking hard, Woo walked in.

"Alright, let's go. I got a car out there."

I rushed over to the window and looked down. There was, in fact, a car parked out there.

"Whose driving?"

"Me."

"You don't know how."

"I'll learn. Here," he tossed a bag at me, "wash him up and put these clothes on him. I'm serious; our days of living like bums are over."

"He doesn't have a name."

"Divine," Woo sighed. "Give him one then." Woo was walking around our section of the building, gathering our things. "Make sure that shit cool, not like mine."

"What I like, Roland, just think when we have babies, we gone name our little girl Rovina," I said, cheesing.

"What, who says I'm having babies with yo young ass?"

"Woo, you two years older than me. The older we get, the less that matters."

Woo shook his head, "go wash up."

I put my hand out to the little boy, and he took it.

"I know what his name is, Woo," I said excitedly.

"What is it, Divine?" Woo asked dryly.

"Million, and I'll call him Milli for short."

Nothing became different with Million around; we still did the same shit. The only difference was we had a lookout, and sometimes he would act to. Woo stayed true to his word. Every night, we slept in a bed, all three of us together. Woo would get us hotel rooms. Sometimes they were nice, and sometimes they were bad, but there was always a bed.

Once Woo decided on the place where we would settle down, I begged him to let Million go to school. He told me repeatedly how hard this would be, seeing as we kind of stole Million from his mom, but I still begged. Woo and I didn't get the chance to have an education or childhood. So I wanted Million to have those things. Woo, as always, made my wish come true. He found a crack head and got her to vouch for Million, and because of the condition she was in, the state believed her. Million officially became Million Carver. He got the paperwork and everything. It was hard as hell getting that crack head clean, but once we got Million's papers, we sent her on her way.

I'm sure you're wondering what this has to do with the hoe comment. But just relax, I'm getting there. So anyway, Woo found a small apartment for us, and it was perfect. I really fell into that young mother role; I did everything for Million while Woo only showed him how to use guns and shit. Woo claimed that they'd be all around the apartment anyway and that Million needed to understand that they weren't toys. Agreeing with Woo, I let the shit show happen.

Woo and I never confirmed or denied our relationship. Woo knew I loved him; he knew I thought the world of him, and that was enough for me. Once our crimes started paying off more, we were able to form a little crew— Woo, our fearless leader and, me, the Divine plan maker. There was an unspoken understanding between Woo and me that I belonged to him and that he belonged to me. Nobody ever questioned it, and neither did we.

At least until we moved, Woo moved us to a better neighborhood. He said the schools in this area would be better for Million. We still lived in an apartment; the only difference was there were two bedrooms. Thinking that he'd finally outgrown me, I began feeling insecure. I'd just turned sixteen and Woo eighteen, so maybe he did want a girlfriend. Woo had never tried anything with me. Sure, we slept in the same bed every night, but he never made a move. Moving into this place meant that we'd probably end up in separate rooms.

"Why you taking yo stuff in Million's room, Divine?" Woo asked tiredly as he moved a couch through the door.

We had the guys over helping us move. We didn't have much, but the more help, the quicker things would go. Million was at school; we planned on surprising him when he got out.

"Huh?" I asked, dumbfounded.

Looking around at the boys, Woo nodded his head towards the door, and they all left.

"Why you moving your stuff in Millions room?"

"I thought that since there are two bedrooms here, one would be mine and the other yours." I was beginning to feel pathetic. I was starting to feel like a twelve-year-old girl again. "Milli and I can just sleep together to give you your space."

Woo didn't say anything. He just walked into Million's room and started taking my stuff out. He took my things and put them in the master bedroom. I stood there looking stupid, watching him. What was he thinking?

"I don't know what kind of fucking girl shit you going through right now, but you are sleeping with me. That's our room over there," he pointed to the room he had just walked out of. "Put yo shit in there."

Then he walked back out of the door to get more things. Just like that, all my worries disappeared. I walked into the room that Woo and I would share, smiling.

"Divine," I heard Woo call my name, "go get Million."

Walking out of the room, I walked over to Woo, and he handed me the car keys.

"Raylo, go with her and come straight back," Woo said, looking at Raylo. I just smiled, nodding my head, then walked out of the door.

My relationship with Woo from then on became clear. I was his woman, his partner, and his companion. We did everything together; we always did everything together. I don't know why I thought things would change. We were abandoned kids that had to grow up fast to survive. We didn't have time to be innocent; we didn't have time to make mistakes and learn from them. Whenever we moved in the streets, everything had to be perfect. No one out there cared about who we were or where we came from. They'd kill us just as quickly as we'd kill them.

Woo and I didn't have sex often; for Woo, sex wasn't serious. We'd grown up watching our mothers do it with different people daily. Woo still had demons he was dealing with, and I was alright with that. I remember having this conversation with Woo. It's one of many that I would never forget. Woo had just turned nineteen, and my seventeenth birthday was around the corner.

"Woo," I said, turning around in his arms, facing him.

"Divine," he answered.

"Do you think I'm ugly?"

Woo smacked his lips and took a deep breath.

"Why would you ask that?"

"I mean, we sleep here every night, and we barely fuck." He sat up and turned the lamp on. Woo ran his hand through his hair.

"Why you always gotta be like that?" he said, looking right at me. I was confused, and I just asked him a question. "Divine, stop talking like that. Sure, we from that, but we don't have to be that. When it comes to you, sex isn't something I need. You know what I want from you, right?"

I was hanging on to his every word. "Loyalty," I answered.

"That's right, sex can come from anywhere, we both know that. But the shit we building, the surviving we doing. I could only do this with you. I can't rest around nobody else like this but you, fuck everybody else. That's why to me, you the most beautiful girl in the world. Stop this peasant talk, Queen," he said, looking at me seriously.

I began smiling. The way I listened to him, you would have thought he was a preacher, and I, his congregation. If Woo told me something, I took it to heart, every word. Outside, we were riffraff, criminals, delinquents, even kidnappers, depending on how you looked at it. But in here, in this fancy little apartment, we were still two kids with a bunch of issues just trying to console each other.

"Divine, I would never lie to you, ever. When I say you a queen, I mean it. We run all this shit. We creating our empire. I'm king, so how could you be anything less? Be confident. We know all too well what happens to woman that walk around the world weak. You will not be weak."

Woo turned around, turned the light back off, then laid down. He pulled me back down to my original spot and held me close.

"Divine, watch yo mouth. Queens are not out here getting fucked."

I started giggling. Woo was right; I needed to work on my confidence. He walked around like he ruled the world, so I couldn't be next to him, falling short. I was far too beautiful; Million told me this every day. Even though I didn't go to school, I could read, and I could write. Woo told me I was smart every chance he got. He told me I was needed and that he wouldn't have made it this far without me. I remember going to sleep that night thinking, when I wake up, I'm going to be a new me.

It was like Woo turned a switch on in me. The timid smiling Divine became no more, as my confidence went through the roof. Woo did nothing but encourage it. I am beautiful, I am a genius and I have this beautiful body. Who would dare look down on me? All this time, I'd been using my body, charms, and voice to get killers, pimps, and pedophiles to follow me. They would follow my every word as I led them to Woo and his gun.

When I turned eighteen, Woo asked me to marry him. He didn't give me a reason why and I didn't ask. He handed me a piece of paper, and I signed. We became legally bonded to each other, nothing else changed. We stopped robbing people and became the people we robbed. Woo wanted more, so branching out and dealing drugs made sense. Then after the drugs came the whore houses. At first, I was apprehensive, but Woo said we'd do things differently.

Our lifestyle became faster and faster. Things around us were moving so fast sometimes it was hard for me to keep up. Just because I'm telling it as if it was easy doesn't mean it was. Woo and I stepped on many toes, took all the street corners; we even recruited from our enemies. We were building, and we had nowhere to go but up. I learned a lot. Even if I wasn't book smart, there wasn't anything I didn't know about the streets. And in the midst of all this chaos, Woo managed to break my heart.

I walked into the warehouse one day, or should I say strutted, and all eyes were on me. I wondered for a second why they were staring, but then I remembered the outfit I had chosen for the day. The mini skirt hugged my hips tightly, slightly rising just enough to not show too much. The narcissist in me is beyond saving. Walking up to the office, I opened the door to see Woo and some girl I'd never seen before standing in the middle of our office. Woo had his hand on her face as if he was just caressing it.

"Woo," I said, pulling my gun out.

"Divine," Woo said, ignoring the pending danger he was about to face.

"Bobby, this is my wife, Divine. Divine, this is Bobby," he said, walking over to his desk and taking a seat.

I looked at him as he nonchalantly sat there. Telling myself that it was ok, that I shouldn't act off emotion right now, I walked over to the couch and took a seat. I kept the gun out just in case I decided to shoot them both. After I took a seat, Woo smirked as if he was proud about something.

"Bobby will be moving into the house."

"Whose house?"

"Our house."

I looked at the girl named Bobby, "how old are you?"

"Eighteen," she said, afraid to look at me.

I looked at Woo as he looked dead at me, we've been married for three years, and now, like right now, he wants to pull this. I came here bearing great news, wanting to tell him that we had created a life together, and here he was pushing me out. I closed my eyes, refusing to cry, not in front of this bitch, never in front of this bitch.

"Woo, what does this mean?" I asked, trying to remain calm.

"This means nothing," he answered, looking at me confused.

"Are you trying to push me out?" I asked as my voice broke.

"What?" he said, pushing off his desk. "Divine."

"Woo," I said, taking a number from his book.

"You are my wife. There isn't a person in the world that could cause me to push you out. How could that be the first thing you think of?"

"Well, this Bobby bitch staring at you with stars in her eyes sure isn't trying to hide the fact that yall have fucked, so I'm confused."

"There isn't anything to be confused about," he got down in front of me, grabbing my hands, "Bobby is coming home with us, to our home." This smug motherfucker. "Don't you have something you want to tell me?"

I looked at him, narrowing my eyes. "Come on, Divine, you know if there is anything in the world that has anything to do with you, I know about it."

So, he knows I'm pregnant.

Ignoring what he just said, "so you can fuck other people now, Woo?"

I needed to focus on one thing at a time; I needed to make sure I understood. Even if he was trying to change the subject, I wanted to stay on topic. He's always trying to use his words to manipulate some damn body.

"It's just sex. Besides, she can be useful in other ways," he said, looking up at me seriously.

Hearing him say that, I remembered what sex meant to him. To Woo, sex was nothing but a means to an end. He didn't think of it as what it was; he didn't see it as a way to connect to another person. He just wanted to bust his nut. After taking a moment to think things through, I decided that I loved this man far too much to not be with him. I had given him all of me already, and if this is how he wanted us to live, then so be it. Fine then, Woo, as always, I wish to be just like you. I'll get rid of these hurt feelings.

"So, I can fuck who I want?" I asked.

I was as serious as he was. If this was going to be life, then I'd live it.

Woo stood and walked back over to his desk. He looked from Bobby then to me.

"If that's what will make you happy, Divine. It's just sex. You and I both know where your home is. If my chains remain wrapped around your heart, I don't need anything else. I will forever be loyal to you, and you will forever be loyal to me. You are my Queen."

Open Love

So back to the question, am I a hoe? No. Woo and I openly fuck who we want while still being devoted to each other. This is just life, and I'm living it. Our marriage hasn't suffered for it; we're both happy, and we're raising our beautiful little girl. Did I forget to mention her earlier? Woo, and I did have that little girl, and I named her Rovina Carver. I love my little caramel drop. She is literally my whole universe, and just like her damn daddy, she knows it. So now that you know more about why things are the way they are, I guess we can continue where we left off.

Walking into our mansion after the meeting, I prepare myself for the rant Woo is about to go on. It never fails. Any time he leaves a place Gavriil was just present, he becomes ridiculous. I have never given Woo or anybody else a reason to believe I'd side with Gavriil over Woo. Just as Woo has always put me first, I've put him first. Milli walks past me, trying to head upstairs and out of the way of the pending war.

"Milli," he stops midway up the stairs, "can you go get Vivi from Rena's?" Without even answering, he runs back down the stairs and out of the door.

One down two to go, I look over at Asia, and she's sitting on the couch waiting for the show to start. Between her and Bobby, she's the least disrespectful. I nod my head towards the kitchen, and she giggles while leaving. I swear that hoe has all the screws loose in her head. Shit, maybe I do too. Asia takes nothing seriously; all she wants to do is party. I turn towards Bobby, who's standing next to Woo. I swear this bitch acts like she wants to be one of his damn body parts.

"Div…," before he can even finish saying my name, I cut him off.

"Put yo dog to rest first," I'm not about to play with them.

Woo got me fucked up, and he knows better. Tell that bitch to go take a nap or something.

"Bobby," Woo says while looking right at me.

Bobby doesn't say a word or make a sound. She just makes her way upstairs without looking back. One thing about Woo, he keeps that psycho hoe in check. In all the years of us all living under the same roof, she has never disrespected me. I know Bobby is in love with Woo. I recognize the way she looks at him. Like any woman, how could I not see this hoe's intentions? I know she's just patiently waiting for her time to shine. I know she only dresses like a guy to prove a point. She is not a damn lesbian; she is just dumb. I don't discuss Bobby with Woo anymore. He made it clear a long time ago that neither of us was going anywhere.

It took me a while, but it became on and popping once I got over my initial hurt. Then there's Asia. She's just having fun. She looks at Woo as a come up and I'm not mad at that. Bobby, on the other hand, wants to take my place. Me and her will never get along. Woo out here living this king life, with his concubines and shit. I'm also sure he has other women outside the house as well, which is why after Rovina was born, we haven't had any more babies; I make him use a condom every time. I know who I'm fucking, but I don't know who he's fucking. I no longer ask.

"Divine, stop fucking Gavriil. You got his nose wide open. That fool truly wants what's mine."

"Stop exaggerating, Woo," I say, trying to blow him off.

Woo didn't care about the things I did outside the house, but for some reason, Gavriil got to him. Gavriil was someone I consistently slept with. I always find myself dialing his number or picking up the phone when he calls. Besides Woo, I've only been with Gavriil and one other person. What can I say? I like what I like. Gavriil's been around for the longest. He knows where my heart belongs and that I will never leave or turn my back on Woo no matter what. Woo is everything. To me, Woo is king.

"Don't play with me, Divine. I'm not fucking joking; I'm fucking serious," Woo says loudly, and I draw back a bit.

"Woo, who the fuck do you think you talking to?" Maybe he thought he was talking to Bobby or something. "Do I tell you who to fuck and who not to fuck, especially with all this in-house pussy you got? Kick the fuck back, you talking to me. I'm Divine."

"I know who yo ass is; I made you," he shouts.

"And I made you, the fuck. You think you made it here by yo motherfucking self," I say, gesturing around our mansion.

"Fuck somebody else, anybody else. You gone make me go to war, Divine."

"Then go to war, Woo. Fight for me. I'll be right beside you like I always am. Where is this insecure ass shit coming from?"

"Divine."

"Woo."

"What the fuck you just say to me?"

"I said why you acting insecure?" I look him up and down. I'm not about to fight any man, Queens don't do that, but Woo knows I will shoot his ass. I'm not twelve anymore, so smacking the wind out of me is not an option.

Woo walks up in my face, "you think I won't kill him." He grabs me by my chin.

I try to force myself away from him, but he won't let me go. I feel like I'm about to punk out. What is he tripping for? Does he think I would choose Gavriil over him?

"You don't trust me?"

Just hearing the words come out of my mouth hurt. Finally freeing myself, I begin pacing around the living room. I am heated at the motherfucking audacity. If I wanted to pull somebody's dick out right here and suck it, I would have all the right. Woo better fucking remember who I am before I hurt his fucking feelings.

I'm still pacing back and forth while deep in thought. I like sex with Gavriil. Why would Woo try to take that from me? This is really making me mad because I know if Woo really wants me to leave Gavriil alone, then I will. But please know I'm cleaning the fucking house; I'm shooting Bobby right in the fucking face, and I'm sending Asia ass to the whore house, fuck them!

"Relax, nobody needs to get shot in the face, and don't hurt my feelings," Woo says, grinning. I look up at him, confused. "Yo ass always get to talking to yourself when you mad. I fucked up, my bad. But Gavriil can't have you Div..."

"Of course, he can't," I say, cutting him off.

Looking into his eyes, hoping he understands that I've been his since I was twelve. Woo's the one that changed the rules; I just followed them.

"I know, I know. I don't even know why I just tripped like that. Come here."

I begin pouting and shaking my head no. I'm still pissed about all that bull shit he just said. The fuck he means he made me, so. Bitch I'm Divine.

"Divine."

"Woo," I answer, giving him all the attitude I can muster.

Woo walks over to me and scoops me up into his arms. I begin giggling like I wasn't just hard-pressed on killing somebody. That's all it takes for me to forgive him. I hate being mad at him. That's mostly why I just submit to his whims and act accordingly. If he wants our marriage to be open, then I'll open it up. But please understand Divine will never stand by and watch you have all the fun.

Woo walks us up to our bedroom and throws me on the bed. He bends over me, ripping my shirt open, then he pulls my skirt down smoothly over my legs. Taking his time, he allows his thumbs to caress my legs as he moves down. Woo's eyes shine in the light as he looks down at me; he's standing at the foot of the bed admiring my body. I lay here smiling up at him; I know he loves what he sees. Woo begins unbuttoning his shirt, and I decide to roll over, giving him a better view of my ass, his favorite part. Chuckling, he goes into his pants pocket, pulling out a condom. He grabs my hips positioning them at his pelvis.

"You ready for me, baby?" Woo asks, knowing the damn answer.

He pulls my thong to the side.

"Always," I manage to get out before my face is forced down into the pillows.

Waking up out of my sleep, I stand yawning and stretching. Picking my phone up, I see I have a couple of missed calls. I woke up alone, as Woo must have gone to take care of the problem. I've been sleeping for a couple of hours; my stomach begins growling. I head to the bathroom to shower and fully wake myself up.

Making my way down to the kitchen, I see Million and Rovina sitting at the counter. It looks like Milli is helping her with her homework.

"Hi, mommy," Vivi says, watching me walk into the kitchen.

"Mhmm," I hum, looking away from her.

She knows better; what kind of greeting is that? Vivi jumps out of her chair, laughing.

"Mommy's a baby," she runs over, hugging me.

"That's right. I'm a big baby, so you have to take care of me, right?"

"That's right," she gives me a kiss on my cheek.

"She better take care of this homework first," Milli says, sounding like somebody's daddy.

Vivi lets me go and goes back to her seat to finish her homework. I walk over to the refrigerator and look for something to cook. I feel like I'm starving; anything would taste good right now. The kitchen door opens, being that it leads to the garage. Woo and his funky bunch walk in.

"Daddy, daddy," Vivi screams excitedly.

Sure, wish I received the same treatment around here. She runs right into his arms. I look over at Milli as he places her school things in her backpack. I look back at the dirty intruders; they look clean enough. I guess the call wasn't that important; there's no blood.

"Yo Divine, Korky said everything's good on his end for whenever you ready," Woo says while lifting Vivi up in the air.

"Yeah ok, then where you coming from if everything's good?" I say, pulling some thawed chicken breast out of the refrigerator.

"We got some new girls," he says, leaving the kitchen with Vivi in his arms.

"Bobby," I call out to her before she can follow Woo.

"Yes."

"Did you get up with Mook?"

"No, his peoples say he ain't been around for a while. I think they're lying, but I got some people on his granny house just in case."

I nod my head. Why can't she ever tell me some shit I want to hear? Bobby and Asia walk out of the kitchen, probably looking for they dick.

"Milli, you and Raylo take care of Korky next week. But wait to the last minute to call him, don't give him any time to set anything up."

"Bet," he answers.

"Be alert. I don't fucking like him. Woo always wanna be somebody damn friend. If anything, and I mean anything look weird, or you feel weird, leave. You and Raylo get the fuck out of there. We can kill Korky's ass later."

"Got it. What you wanna do about Mook?" Milli asks.

I take a deep breath, "I guess I'm going to have to give him a visit." I begin seasoning the chicken. "Milli," he looks over at me, "do you think I'm going soft?"

Milli begins laughing, "no. I think Mook got a death wish."

I sigh, "he has to, right? Him not giving me my money can only mean that."

"You want me to find him?"

"Nope," I say, popping the 'p.' "I want that bitch to find him. That's her damn job, right? That's one of the ways she's useful."

"Ma," Milli calls out, and I look over at him, "you sound bitter," he says before standing and walking out of the kitchen.

"You sound bitter," I say, mocking him.

Maybe I am. That bitch is hard at work trying to get Woo to turn against me. As conniving as I am, I see her dumb ass coming from a mile away. Here's a question though, if it truly came down to it, would Woo choose me over her? I guess it doesn't matter; I could run all this shit by myself. It would super suck to do it without Woo though. This was our dream; we dreamt up this shit together. I feel arms snake around my waist.

"What you thinking so hard about?" Woo asks.

I can feel his breath on my ear.

"Who says I was in here thinking?" I ask, smiling.

"You always thinking and plotting. That's why yo head so damn big."

"Shut up. My head not big. It fits my body perfectly. With yo rude ass."

"Whatever you say, Queen Divine," he whispers.

"I love you," I lay my head back on his shoulder.

Woo gives me a kiss on my cheek, "I love yo crazy ass too."

Nah, he wouldn't pick that hoe over me. Bitch I'm Divine.

Happy Birthday

Waking up to my caramel drop jumping up and down on my bed, I can't help but smile. I grab her hugging her tightly.

"Mommy, I can't breathe," she says, laughing.

I begin tickling her, "what are you doing in mommy's bed. Where's everybody?"

"Daddy left last night after kissing me good night. Milli left this morning to meet gork." I guess she's trying to say Korky.

"So, you came to see me, your third choice," I say, pouting.

"Mommy," she pulls my head to her chest as if she's consoling me, "it's your birthday. Happy birthday," she says, getting excited again.

I grab my phone, looking at the date. I guess it is. How did I forget? Picking Vivi up, we head downstairs to find us some breakfast. Walking through the house, it's mad quiet. I guess everybody is gone. I wonder if Woo forgot.

"What do you want for breakfast? Since it's mommy's birthday, we can eat something sweet and yummy."

"I want...," she places her hand on her chin as she thinks. "I want strawberry French toast."

"French toast it is," I begin gathering the things for breakfast.

Vivi jumps up and runs out of the kitchen. Moments later, she returns with a paper in her hand.

"Look, mommy, I drew you a picture for your birthday," Vivi shouts as I flip the first batch of French toast.

Taking the picture from her, I can't help smiling. She drew a picture of me standing tall, looking down on everyone with a crown on my head. Or at least that's how she explained it. I found myself getting a bit irritated. Even my five-year-old child knows I'm a Queen. So why the fuck was Mook testing me like this? Bobby still has not found him; I am beginning to think she's doing this on purpose. The kitchen door opens, pulling me out of my thoughts.

"You were right," Milli says, walking in with Raylo behind him.

"Yo, that shit was fuck...," Before Raylo could finish his sentence, Milli elbows him. "Oh, my bad. Korky real snake-like."

Vivi runs right into Milli's arms. I continue cooking.

"What happen?"

"Million and I got to the spot like two hours early. We were just sitting and waiting as you said. Then we saw the feds pull up," Raylo says, taking a seat.

"How the feds know about the place if I just called dude last night?" Milli asks, looking at me with wide eyes.

"They could have had his phone tapped," I answer, grabbing plates out of the cabinet.

Raylo and Milli look at each other. I go to the fridge to get some whipped cream and strawberries.

"That's the same thing I said to Million, so we wait to see what happens next," Raylo says.

I begin cutting the strawberries up while listening.

"Korky got out of one of the vans," Milli adds.

I sit three plates of French toast on the counter. I dress Vivi up just the way she likes them. She jumps out of Million's arms then walks back over to her seat.

"Woo?" I ask, watching them eat.

"I didn't call him. Figured I would give you the honor of telling him," Milli says with his mouth full.

I grab some napkins and hand them to him.

"The phone you used to call Korky last night?"

"Tossed it in the river," Milli answers.

I nod my head.

"Oh, boss lady, Happy birthday," Raylo manages to say in between chews.

"Thank you," I smile.

I grab my picture and begin walking out of the kitchen; I've lost my appetite. Before I can make my way upstairs, I hear Milli calling me.

"Ma."

I turn to face him. He's holding his hand out with a box in it. I smile at him taking it. Opening the box, it's a diamond bracelet. Milli knows my taste, and I love it.

"Thank you," I playfully punch him on his shoulder.

"Happy birthday," he says, walking back into the kitchen.

I head up to my bedroom, and I sit my picture and the box on my dresser. I walk over to my side of the bed, looking down at my phone. I wonder if Woo tried to call me while I was making breakfast. Picking my phone up, I see I have no missed calls. Just a couple of text messages from some of my guys telling me happy birthday. Rolling my eyes, I dial Woo's number.

Woo answers on the first ring, "Divine."

"Woo, where are you?"

"We got some new pets. I'm making sure they transition properly." Woo is speaking in code.

"All night?" I ask, needing answers.

"All night Divine," he answers, sounding frustrated.

I smack my lips, "well, when are you coming home? I wan…" He cuts me off.

"When I get there. It's some cold babies out here; I gotta help get them warm."

Basically, the young boys on our corners fucking up.

"Send someone else," I say through gritted teeth. I know this fool didn't forget my damn birthday.

"You know how people feel when you just write a check for these things. I have to go personally, show my face. Show them some sincerity, so they know it's real."

Feeling my anger reaching its peak, I decide to just let it go. If Woo wants to forget my birthday, then so be it. If he doesn't want to spend it with me, then fuck him.

"Enjoy," I say, hanging up.

I didn't even say 'I love you,' as I always say that.

Throwing my phone on my bed, I go sit at my vanity and look at myself in the mirror. You are strong, Divine. Calm down, Divine, don't flip on him. You guys shouldn't be arguing; you hate arguing. I sit here repeatedly telling myself to relax till I get up to call his dumb ass back. Before I can even dial Woo's number, I receive a text.

"To the greatest gift God could ever give, Happy Birthday love."

The message is from Gavriil. I feel the smile on my face as I look over at the mirror. The person looking back at me is blushing like some schoolgirl. Running my hands through my hair, I fall back on my bed. I take a deep breath; I feel my heartbeat picking up. I look at the text message again. Why does he make his way into my world at times like these? I dial Woo's number; I'll just tell him to bring his ass home cause it's my birthday and I want to spend it with him.

He doesn't answer. Now I'm looking at my phone in disbelief. I begin laughing to myself. I redial his number; this time, it goes straight to voice mail. So, I take this to mean that Woo won't mind me spending my birthday with someone else. If this was five years ago, I'm sure I'd be somewhere crying, but it isn't. I look at myself again in the mirror as I dial a number that I know is sure to answer my call. My eyes look like they want to let the tears fall, but I won't let them.

"I am honored," Gavriil says, answering the phone.

"Of course, you are," I say, faking confidence while still staring at my sad self. "Can I borrow some time?"

"Always," he answers quickly. "My time is yours to have."

I watch as I smile at his words. "Fucking flirt," I say, not letting him hear how flattered I truly am. "I'll be leaving my house in forty-five minutes. Send me your location by then." I hang up.

Putting my phone back on the charger, I go to shower and get changed. Woo wishes I would sit in the house and cry over him on my birthday. Not I and not today. I didn't even get to tell him about his snitch-ass friend. Stepping out of the shower, I go into my closet. Usually, I would take my time, but I just feel like running out of here right now. It's like the longer I stay in the house, the more pathetic I feel. The queen will never be pathetic. Today I'll dress casually. I'll pull one of Bobby's numbers and wear some jogging pants. I'm sure I won't be dressed for long anyway.

Gavriil likes when I dress comfortably around him. He tells me all the time that the makeup and heels are just a mask I choose to hide behind. Maybe he's right, but if I wasn't dressed like that in the first place, he wouldn't have wanted to fuck me the first time. I decide to wear my real hair out today as well; you'd think it's his damn birthday. Taking out my protective style is easy, it's just four braids. I moisturize my hair then grab my jacket.

I don't even look in the mirror as I leave because I know I look a hot ass mess. Walking down the stairs, I see Milli and Vivi in the living room.

"Hey Milli."

Milli looks at me. Then his eyes move up and down, taking in my clothes. He stands up.

"Are you about to go to the gym?"

I smile.

"Something like that." It's not a lie. I plan on having a workout. "Can you watch Vivi? If you have to leave, just drop her to Rena. I already talked to her, and she said if I need her today, she can watch her. I have her bag packed in her closet. If you take her there, just text me, and I'll pick her up."

"It's cool. I don't have anything happening right now. If something come up, I'll let you know," he sits back down on the couch.

"Bye Vivi. Mommy loves you," I say, walking out of the door.

Getting into my car, I sit for a second, taking a deep breath; maybe I should just stay home. Then when Woo walks his stupid-looking ass in the house, I can cuss him out. My phone vibrates, letting me know I have a notification. It's Gavriil. He just sent me an address with a room number, and it's some fancy hotel. Fuck it, I'm going. I send Bobby a text letting her know I'm leaving and that Milli has Vivi. I curse myself for texting that hoe's phone. I just want her to tell Woo I want him to call me and apologize. I want him to tell me he's sorry for forgetting and to come back home so he can make it up to me. I'm always giving him openings like this. I don't want to drive into Gavriil's arms; I want to be in Woo's.

Woo has me fucked up though, just because I want to be sad doesn't mean that I'll do it. I'm not the same punk-ass little girl. Now I have all the nerve in the world. Pulling up to the valet of the fancy hotel, I reach under my seat, pulling out a perfume. Gavriil gave it to me; he said the moment he smelled it, he could only imagine it being on my skin. I almost never wear it for him, and I'm sure Woo would trip if he knew Gavriil bought it. I would never take it inside the house, so it lives right here up under my car seat.

A younger guy walks over to my car's driver's side door; he has a big smile on his face. I step out, handing him my keys. I give him a wink, then place my sunglasses on. Making my way through the hotel lobby, I walk as if I see and hear no one. Pretending not to be nervous in front of others is something I've become used to. Once I get on the elevator, I press the button that will lead me to the penthouse. Gavriil never fails at going all out. We could have just gotten a regular room.

Once I reach my destined floor, the elevator doors open, and Gavriil's men stand before me.

"We have to search you," a guard that I've never seen before says.

"Try it and see if my blade stays tucked and not in your windpipe," I'm looking straight ahead.

As if I'd allow this fucker to touch me.

"Igor, leave her," I hear a familiar voice.

Smirking, I step off the elevator. Viktor is standing there waiting for me.

"Hey Vik, it's been a while," I begin smiling.

I like Viktor. He is Gavriil's best friend and right-hand man. He is also nice to me, so we get along.

"Divine, beautiful as always," he says, leading me to the room door.

Viktor pulls the key out of his pocket. Opening the door, he steps to the side so I can walk in. Hearing the door close behind me, I take my sunglasses off. I begin looking around the room. As always, this is just too much. Sitting my purse down on a table, I walk over to the balcony, looking at the view. I take a deep breath, Divine what are you doing here?

"The enchanting beauty herself graces me with her presence," his voice warms my ears. I turn around with a smile on my face.

Gavriil walks out on the balcony with me shirtless. Why is this man so pleasing to my eyes? Gavriil and his way with words, this man was basically a damn poet. He looks over my appearance taking it all in, the smirk on his face turning into a smile. Once he's in front of me, I stare straight into his eyes. I refuse to let him know the true effect he has on me.

"Happy Birthday," he says in a whisper.

"You said that alre...," before I can finish my sentence, his lips are already on mine.

He has one hand holding the side of my face while the other is wrapped around my neck. He thinks he's slick, but I know he does this to control the flow of our kiss. I like to go hard and fast, while he likes to go slow, taking his time savoring it. I usually don't kiss like this, not even Woo, but Gavriil just forces me into his world. Pulling away from me, he looks down at me. I'm sure my eyes are filled with passion.

He takes my hand, leading me to the bedroom. I don't even look around to admire the décor. I try taking my shirt off, but he stops me.

"Tsk tsk tsk, don't you dare." Stepping close to me again, I feel his hands grab my hips. "I'll do it."

Lifting my arms up, I allow him to pull my shirt over my head. My heart is beating fast, and the adrenaline flowing through me right now is causing me to lose my breath. I don't like waiting, and Gavriil always makes me wait. He loves taking his time. Looking down at him, I watch as he gets down on his knees, pulling my pants and underwear with him. Looking up at me with those dazzling blue eyes, he pushes his face into my core.

I don't know how it happened or when, but I find myself lying with my back on the bed. When did he pick me up and put me here? I know for a fact that his lips haven't left the ones between my legs. Was it before or after my second orgasm? He's always like this; Gavriil is always trying his best to get me to lose my mind. I can't take this anymore; I pull on his hair, pulling him up to me.

"Fucking tease," I say while kissing and biting his lips.

"You know I love it when you beg. It's only at moments like this when you're honest," he begins attacking my neck.

I reach down and start unbuttoning his pants, fuck is these still on for anyway?

"No marks Gavriil, Woo will kill your ass," I say as I rush, getting his pants off. He doesn't say anything. He just chuckles.

"Slow down, Divine," he pushes off me to finish taking his clothes off.

I don't care how I look right now. As soon as his shirt comes off, I pull him back down, wrapping my legs around him. My body is so fucking desperate right now, and he knows it. He has that beautiful ass smile on his face; I hate this man. Without any help or guidance, his dick finds its place. Gavriil pushes into me, causing me to close my eyes.

"Open them and look at me," Gavriil says through gritted teeth.

I open my eyes; why did I do that? This is when I feel the most vulnerable with him. Whenever we have sex, his eyes are always looking right into mine. I know there are so many things he's trying to express to me, things he can't say because I won't let him. I feel my whole-body shiver beneath him. Gavriil never goes at the pace I want him to, and he never switches positions. We're always just like this. Him on top of me, moving slowly, stirring my body into a shaking mess, with his eyes on mine.

I always feel like time has stopped. He makes it so that all I see and feel is him. No matter how many times I beg, he never goes faster or harder. When I leave him, I always get mad at myself for allowing the sex to be so boring, but I always come back. I always end up right here, right where he wants me. Feeling my body ready for release, I dig my fingers into his back. It never happens the way I want it to, but with Gavriil, it always happens. I find myself biting into his shoulder. Even if I want to yell out his name, I won't allow myself to. There it is, the release that keeps me coming back for more.

Gavriil thrusts into me a bit faster; I fucking hate him. Pulling himself out of me, he releases on my leg. I lay there on the bed with shaking legs doing the best I could to catch my breath. He walks into the bathroom, turns the shower on, then comes out with a wet rag to wipe off his dead babies. Then he helps me stand, and we walk into the bathroom to shower together.

"When will you stop with this boring shit, Gavriil?" I ask.

"Tell that to the women who needed help out of bed." I smack my lips because he's not lying. "The kind of love you want from me is not the kind of love you need from me."

I roll my eyes while turning him around so I can scrub his back. I do not want to hear his sweet words right now. Sex with Gavriil makes me feel a bit guilty. It's as if we're always making love.

"Gavriil, you don't know what I need," the confidence in my voice has gone.

"Then why are you here on your birthday, beautiful?"

I don't say anything, because why am I here? I should be at home with my beautiful little girl, my wonderful son, and my perfect husband. We should be celebrating me. I want to feel like the only girl in the world, even if it's for one day. Not liking my silence, Gavriil turns to face me.

"You're always this way, Divine. You hold everything in until you can't anymore, then you show up in front of me with tears in your eyes," he raises his hand to my face, wiping a tear off it.

Fuck, I hate my fucking self. Moving his hand off my face, I let the water hit my face, just to wash the tears away. Gavriil shakes his head then steps out of the shower. I don't have time for this shit. Not today, Gavriil, please not today.

"Go home, Divine. I'm on the verge of just taking you and locking you up. I'll keep you all to myself."

"Gavriil," I say, rinsing the soap off my body.

"No, don't call my fucking name." He's pissed; his accent is coming out. "You think I like sharing you?"

I step out of the shower, "you're not the one sharing me. I belong to Woo." I grab a towel and begin drying myself off. "I need my purse."

Pissed, he walks out of the bathroom. Seconds later, he walks back in with my purse. Going through it, I grab my lotion.

"Divine, why are you fucking me?"

I smile, "what we do can't be considered fucking, Gavi," I'm trying to lighten up the mood. "Besides, why can't I fuck you?"

I look into his eyes. I can tell he's really pissed.

"Why can't we ever end things on a good note? Why does it have to end like this every time?" I ask.

He steps into my face, "you know why. Divine, you know what I want from you. You know how I feel. Tell me how I'm supposed to react to your tears."

"I've never promised you anything. I love my husband; I will always choose him." Gavriil is pissing me off. If you feel like this, then stop answering my damn calls.

Gavriil kisses my forehead, "of course you will, Divine." He walks out of the bathroom. Then I hear the bedroom door slam shut.

I look at myself in the mirror. I need to get my shit together. Gavriil is not my man; I don't even understand why I entertain his bullshit. I grab my phone out of my purse, no missed calls. Woo still hasn't called me. I feel myself getting angry. It's my birthday. Why is everyone acting like bitches? I text Milli telling him to get Vivi ready, that I'm on my way to pick them up. I'll just hang out with my kids. What the fuck did I start crying for?

After fixing my hair and getting dressed, I walk out of the bedroom. It looks like Gavriil is having some sort of meeting. All eyes are on me.

"Gentlemen," I say, walking past them all. Gavriil is sitting on the couch with a scowl on his face, still gorgeous, still shirtless. I run my hand over his shoulder as I walk out.

"I'll call you," I say in a low, seductive voice.

"Of course, you will," he says, still pissed. I smile, walking out of the door.

New Girl

Walking into the house with my hands full, I see we have an audience in the kitchen. Bobby, Asia, and Woo are all sitting at the counter, looking at me. I smile brightly.

"Hey!" I say, then I sit the bags down and go back into the garage to get the rest of our stuff.

Milli and I went overboard as we always do. Shopping is literally the best therapy, plus it is my birthday. Milli is getting the very tired Vivi out of her car seat; he walks in behind me.

"Daddy," she says as soon as she sees Woo. He stands, taking her out of Milli's arms.

Woo takes Vivi upstairs, more than likely to lay her down. We wore her out, and she's going to be asleep through the whole night.

"Yall need some help?" Asia asks, watching me and Milli walk in and out.

"Nope," I say, out of breath. I need to start back working out. We are just bringing the shit in the house. I still have to sort through it and put this shit up. "We got it. You just sit right there and relax."

"That's all of it," Milli says, walking in with the last of our bags.

I look up at him smiling. I am truly happy at the moment.

It took me some time, but I put everything into perspective. I got some birthday dick; I got gifts from my babies. Plus, I got to spend the day with them shopping and eating junk. Today was a good day. Milli got to walk around with me and act like the kid he is, though he still had his piece on him. We just spent a regular day out, no drama.

I take a seat on the floor in front of all the bags.

"Milli, Imma sit all Vivi stuff right here," I point to a spot on the floor, "when you catch your breath, just start taking them up to her room. Sit the stuff in her closet. I gotta go through it and start getting rid of the stuff she can't fit anymore."

"Alright," he says, taking a seat at the counter.

Woo walks into the kitchen. He nudges Milli on his shoulder.

"Can't speak, little nigga? Don't think just cause you growing up that I won't put your ass on the ground," Woo says playfully to Milli while ruffling his hair.

"Alright, you got it, you king. Please stop." Milli is trying to push his hands away, "how are you? How was your day?"

"My day was the same ole same ole. What happen to that thing yo momma told you to take care of?"

Milli looks right at me, and I shrug my shoulders. "He wasn't answering his phone, so I couldn't tell him."

"Tell me what?" Woo says, looking back and forth between Milli and me.

"He the feds." Milli stands and starts taking Vivi's things up to her room.

Woo looks at me, but I ignore him and continue sorting through the bags. I don't feel like arguing tonight. Milli's shoes are piling up; he's going to get his shit next.

"Divine."

"Woo."

He begins laughing, "what? You not gone say I told you so?"

"I am not. I'm just happy that my son has enough sense to listen to me. If he and Raylo didn't get there early, we'd be trying to bail him out of jail," I say dryly.

Ignoring my attitude, Woo exclaims, "man, fuck Korky! I'm gone murder his bitch ass when I see him."

"No, you not, Woo. He with the feds. For right now, don't do anything. Just make some shit up and tell him we couldn't get the money together in time or something."

"He didn't seem like a fed," Asia says, looking shocked.

I just start shaking my head.

"What do the feds look like?" Milli asks, coming into the kitchen to grab more things.

"I don't know. They just have a vibe," she answers.

Woo walks over to her and grabs her by the chin, "and this is why I don't let you do the thinking around here."

Milli laughs while on his way out of the kitchen.

"Fuck you, Woo," she shouts, pulling away from him.

"So are we just going to let him roam free?" Bobby asks, looking at me.

"No, Bobby, I'll take care of it." Why is this hoe questioning me? Just hearing her voice is fucking irritating. I stop sorting the stuff and look at her, "where's Mook?" Questioning me, I got a question for your ass.

She looks away from me, "I still got my people on his grandma house. He hasn't been through there yet."

I smirk, "it's good, Bobby, don't worry about it. I'll take care of him too. I'll just clean up all the mess like I always fucking do."

I asked this bitch to do one thing. I thought Woo said the hoe was fucking useful.

"Divine," Woo says. I ignore him and finish sorting the bags.

Surprisingly I didn't get myself anything. Vivi and Milli got most of the stuff. Then I bought the three dummies a couple of things.

Milli walks back into the kitchen.

"Yo Woo, I thought you wanted to ask Milli..." I cut Bobby's ass off before she can finish.

"Ask him about what?" I say, looking between her and Woo.

See, everything this hoe does irks my soul.

"Oh yeah, Million," Woo says, looking at Milli, "I paid the credit card bill today. What the fuck you out here buying?"

Before Milli could answer, "why she has to remind you to ask about that?" I ask Woo.

"She was right there when I was paying it off my phone. So, I asked her to remind me to ask him about it."

"Yeah, ok," I say, pissed the fuck off.

Don't have this hoe questioning my son about shit. He can do whatever the fuck he wants with that damn card. That's why I gave it to him. Woo ass is not fucking slick either. The only reason he paid that bill was so he could see what the fuck I'm buying. There's no other reason for him to be paying it. The cards are in Milli's and my name. Deciding I don't want to be mad, I let it go.

"Asia, this stuff right here is yours," I point to her pile. "Bobby, that's your stuff, and Woo, that shit right there is yours."

Asia rushes over to her stuff, going through the bags.

"This is so fucking cute. We should go out tonight," she gushes, looking at Woo.

I stand up off the floor and walk over to the fridge. I guess he said no or something because she begins whining.

"Man, it's Saturday. Why should we stay in the house?" she asks.

I go take a seat in my kitchen nook while looking at the show. It's always entertaining to watch Woo interact with his hoe's. He ignores her and looks over at me.

"Divine, where did you go earlier?" I guess I count as one too.

"We went to the mall, got food," I answer.

"Don't play with me. You told Bobby that Million had Vivi and that you were going out."

I begin staring at Woo. So he got my message and still didn't call me. It's like nobody want me to be calm today. Everybody wants me to act out on my birthday.

"Well," he says, waiting for my answer.

"I went to see Gavriil, then I came home, picked up my kids and went out," I make sure I'm looking right at him as I speak calmly.

Woo begins rubbing his chin while looking at me. I know he wants to act a fool, but he can't, especially not with dumb and dumber next to him. I have never lied to Woo, and I don't plan on starting. Whenever he gets pissed at me, he gets quiet and starts rubbing his beard while staring at me. He looks away from me and back over to Milli.

"You never did answer my question."

"I bought a bracelet," Milli answers.

"A bracelet," Woo says, "I know you ain't out here tricking on no young hoe."

I shake my head at Woo's dumbass. Milli is not him; he would never trick on a random girl. I taught Milli a long time ago to take love and sex seriously. I believe that if you are fucking somebody, you're giving a little of yourself to that person. Which is why I keep picking the phone up for Gavriil. Well, that and other things. I hear my phone ringing, so I walk over to my purse, pulling it out.

"I bought the bracelet for Ma. Today's her birthday," Milli says, shaking his head and walking out of the kitchen with the last of his things.

My eyes are stuck on Woo as I answer the phone.

"Hello."

"Boss lady, we got a problem at the Village," Raylo says through the phone.

Woo's eyes are looking into mine, and I watch as he goes through a series of emotions. Deciding I don't want to wait to see which one he settles on, I grab my purse.

"I'm on my way," I hang up my phone and place it in my purse.

"I'll be back I say, looking at Woo.

"Divine," Woo says.

"I'll take care of this one. You been at it all day; get some rest," I walk out of the kitchen and get in my damn car.

I pull into The Raven Village homes. The complex consists of three large five-story buildings. Whenever I come here, I can't help but feel accomplished. This was the first huge purchase Woo and I ever made. We bought the land, which was a hassle. The city didn't want to give it to us because we were young and black, but as always, Woo made it happen. We own many properties around the city and some out of state, but this one is closest to my heart.

I remember working super hard to get the money we needed to build the buildings, making sure that we created something for low-income families that wasn't trash. The Village is beautiful, and I made sure that the people that moved in knew that there are expectations they have to uphold. It's a wonderful place to raise children; I had Woo put a playground right in the middle. There are schools right up the street, grocery stores around the corner; it's perfect. The only complaint one would make is that there aren't any police stations close, but around here, Woo and Divine serve as the police.

There are no drugs in the Village because I decided I wanted to allow families to live in the apartments. I told Woo no drugs. There is this thing called compromise in marriage, so I had to make one of our buildings a hoe house. It's only one building, and my system is full fucking proof.

I don't treat my girls like shit, and everyone has a choice. They say the Village is like a hoe paradise. I run the Village. Woo runs the other houses, and how he does things is completely different from mine. According to him, I spend too much money rather than making it, yet every time we go over the books, The Village comes out on top. My girls are all clean and beautiful; I make sure they're checked and safe.

I keep them protected at all hours of the day, and no business is conducted outside of the building. As soon as you walk in, there is a check-in desk. At the desk, you discuss what you're interested in then they make recommendations based on what you ask for; the higher you go up, the nastier the girls get. I have two managers and guards all over the place. The Village is literally running like a business. Selling pussy is so fucking lucrative it doesn't make sense.

Rent is collected monthly, and the women are paid weekly, like at a regular job. The split is 70/30, them seventy me thirty. This is where Woo and I disagree. He does 40/60;

that's too much to be taking from someone. I take thirty percent off the top of whatever they make, they set their own prices and if they can pay their rent at the end of the month, they can stay. I have a doctor come out to do weekly checkups and drug tests. I'm strict, but I believe I'm reasonable.

My clientele is VIP; most are powerful men with money that come through the city and stop by the Village. It's a place that can be trusted. Like I said, I take care of my girls, so they take care of me. Everything is done discreetly and cleanly, which is bringing me to a crossroads. How could there be a problem? I pull up to the valet, and Raylo runs over to the driver's side of my car, opening my door.

"Sorry about this. Marcia called me, and I didn't know how to handle it," he says, panicked.

"Handle what, Raylo?" I ask, walking into the building.

Marcia runs up to me before Raylo can begin explaining. I look behind her and see two men in suits with their guns pulled. I sigh.

"Divine, Mayor Hawkins showed up unannounced and just walked into the new girls' room."

"What do you mean just walked in? Where were you, Marcia?" I ask, looking at her desk. I have her there for a fucking reason.

"I had to use the restroom," she says, looking down.

"Ok, so then where the fuck was Brandon? I put his big ass in the lobby for a reason." She doesn't answer me. I don't have time for this.

"Raylo, go look at the cameras to see why the fuck my lobby was empty." He jogs away. "Finish telling me what happened."

"Well, the new girl told Mayor Hawkins that she was only giving blow jobs, and he didn't like that. I guess he slapped her, so she pulled her knife on him. Now she has her knife to his throat, and those guards have their guns pulled on her. I didn't know what to do, so I called Raylo."

I walk away from her. Everyone fucking sucks today. I walk past the guards and into the apartment. I look around; the place looks nice. I wonder how she's managed to stay here while only sucking dick.

"Divine, thank god you're here. Get this bitch off me," Mayor Hawkins says.

I walk over to her couch and take a seat; she is a very pretty girl. I begin checking her out.

"Hawkins, what are you doing down here?" I glare at him.

"I... I... I made a mistake. I did a couple of lines before coming here."

"And you're sober now?" I ask.

"I kind of didn't have a choice," he laughs nervously.

I look over at the pretty new girl, "what's your name?"

She looks at me, not sure of what she should do. "Gucci," she answers. "This pink mothafucka owe me a damn apology. I said no, and he put his hands on me. I don't play that fucking shit."

I smile; I like her.

"How long have you been here, Gucci?"

"Two months," she answers.

"How old are you?"

"Seventeen." I close my eyes and take a deep breath.

All day, all damn day, mothafuckas have been testing me.

"Alright Gucci, let Hawkins go and come go for a ride with me," I say, smiling, but I am burning up on the inside.

"You just gone get big dude over there to kill me," she says.

I look over and see that Raylo is finished with the task I gave him.

"Well, Gucci, I'm Divine; nice to meet you. I'm sure you've heard about me. I will not be hurting you or letting anyone else hurt you."

She begins cursing herself, calling herself stupid. Then she lets him go.

"That's it, Divine?" Mayor Hawkins yells.

I glare at him while standing, and he takes a step back.

"Hawkins, first you ignore my rules, then you put your hands on one of my girls. I should kill you and these dumbass guards. Not to mention she's a fucking minor."

"I'm sorry, Divine," he says like a fucking coward.

"Not me, Hawkins."

He looks at Gucci, "I'm sorry." She looks at him smiling.

"Gucci, go pack your shit up," I say, making the smile fall off her face.

"But I thought..." I put my hand up, stopping her.

I don't let Milli back talk me; I'm sure as hell not about to let her. She walks back into the bedroom.

"Hawkins, take yo pasty ass upstairs to Lauren, where you should have been in the first place."

He gathers his things then walks out of the apartment. I look over at Raylo, ready to break his fucking jaw.

"Why the fuck is a seventeen-year-old in my damn building?"

"Woo told me to put her here two months ago. I didn't know how old she was," he answers, ready for whatever I'm about to throw at him.

"Two months ago, fool, she been in my building for two fucking months." I pull my phone out to call Woo's raggedy ass, but it's fucking dead. Great.

I walk out of the apartment and into the lobby. I see Brandon has reemerged and found his fucking post.

"What the fuck was these mothafucks doing, Raylo?"

Before Raylo could answer me, Brandon stepped over to me.

"Boss lady, me and Marcia been seeing each other." Feeling all the anger I've been pushing down reaching its peak, I punch Brandon right in his fuckin nuts. He falls to the ground holding his dick. Good thing I have on gym shoes. I kick him as hard as I can in his fucking stomach.

I look over at Marcia. "Let this shit happen again, I fucking dare you, bitch. I will put a bullet in both of yall fucking heads."

"Boss lady," Raylo says.

"Shut yo ass up. I should definitely shoot you." I'm just confused right now. Why is the world trying me? "Raylo, put Brandon's ass on the day shift. Have these horny fucks work different shifts. Brandon, get yo ass up off the ground." Brandon struggles but manages to get up.

"Thank you," he says in gratitude. This is what I mean, they know I don't play this bullshit, so why are they trying me? Marcia's ass is at her desk crying. I gotta get out of here. They both better be lucky. I don't want to kill nobody on my birthday.

"Raylo, go get my fucking car." I feel myself getting a headache. Raylo jogs out of the building.

Gucci walks over to where I'm standing, "where are you taking me?"

"To my house. I don't know what the fuck Woo was thinking when he sent you here. My phone is dead, so I can't call him. I need to get to the bottom of all this bullshit."

Run me my Money!

"Your house is beautiful," Gucci says, looking out of the window.

"Thank you."

"I didn't even know Woo had a wife. I thought he was fucking that gay girl," she says as we travel up my driveway and into the garage.

"He is," I say, turning the ignition off and stepping out of the car.

Walking into the kitchen, I see they've moved the party.

"Woo," I yell out loudly.

I walk over to the fridge and grab bottled water. Today has been a day. I look over at the clock, and it's two in the fucking morning.

Woo walks into the kitchen, and his eyes find Gucci's first. He looks from her over to me, "what happen?"

Using both my arms to hold my body up on the counter, I just look at him. How should I come at him? Should I smile and speak calmly or stay true to myself and go knock the shit out of him?

"So, fuck my business," I say, deciding to speak calmly.

"No, Divine. I need her to make back the money her mother owes me."

"So why put her in my building? You have all those fucking houses. Why send her to the Village?"

"She would make my money back faster there. Shit, she has been making it back," he says, walking over to the pantry.

"Woo, I promise. I don't want to argue. But the way you are dismissing how you have me fucked up is really pissing me off. This child is seven fucking teen. I know yo ass knew that. Having her young ass in a place where my clients trust me is a bomb waiting to explode."

"She's almost done anyway," he says, nonchalant as always.

"Then why didn't you tell me in the first place?" I'm glaring at him now. "You knew I would say no. I don't have underage pussy in my building. You are selfish and don't give a fuck about nobody but your fucking self.

"I only care about myself, Divine?" he asks, getting a bit louder. "I'm selfish?" he begins laughing. "I can't be too selfish. I'm sharing yo ass with half the fucking town."

I look over at Gucci, who's standing up against the wall, confused and not knowing what she just walked into.

"You wanna talk about who getting shared around this bitch…" Woo cuts me off.

"You spent your birthday with Gavriil," now he's yelling. Why is that a problem? I'm confused.

"Because you fucking forgot. I called your stupid ass, and you turned your phone off. The fuck was I supposed to do?"

"Not be out fucking a whole other nigga and one you know I got friction with."

Here we go, "fuck you, Woo. You forgot about me, not the other way around. Then you got a minor in my hoe house like the police won't shut my shit down. Don't try to turn this on me. You fucked up."

Milli walks into the kitchen, "Ma, yall gone wake Vivi up."

I take a deep breath, trying to calm down.

"Woo, the rules of our relationship were laid out by you. I refuse to sit in the house on my birthday crying over some shit I agreed to. You wanna fuck dumb and dumber, so be it. But understand I'm Divine. Just like you got options, I do too." I look back at Gucci. "Don't ever do no shit like this again. I don't fuck with your businesses, don't fuck with mine. As far as Gavriil goes, it's just sex, right?"

Woo doesn't say anything else; he stares at me. Deep down inside, he knows I'm right. He can't do that pimp shit with me because I'm a pimp too. I'm not out here fucking just anybody. Call me what you want, but I'm always looking up. Woo knows, just like I know that Gavriil is a couple of steps up from him. Woo tries, but he knows he'll never be able to control me like he does Bobby.

Deciding that this conversation is over, I look at Milli, "take this girl to a room. I'm tired."

Milli walks over to her introducing himself; I roll my eyes. He sounds just like Woo. The two of them walk out of the kitchen, and I'm shocked. She gave me shit when I tried to bring her here. Now she's just following Milli. I start to head up to my bedroom.

"Divine," I stop in my tracks, "I wasn't finished talking."

I turn, facing Woo.

"I know what 'just sex' looks like. If it was just sex between you and him, I wouldn't be this pissed." He starts rubbing his chin while looking at me. "You like him, don't you?"

I stare in amazement. I am fucking amazed. Whose mans is this?

"Woo, fuck you. Fuck you for not remembering my birthday, fuck you for not apologizing and fuck you again for not saying Happy Birthday. That crazy bitch got your head all confused. I'm tired of you questioning me about someone I barely see, as two bitches that didn't come out of my pussy sleep in my house every day. I have accepted that our childhoods fucked us up, and I have accepted that this is the best relationship we can manage because of it. You brought in all these extras when I should have been the star. I never wanted to fuck anybody else. All I wanted was you."

"So why you fucking him?"

"Really, Woo. I'm fucking him to keep up with you. I'm not sitting around waiting for you. He remembered my birthday, he thought about me. Where were you?" Without even realizing it, tears are coming down my face. This is why

I hate talking about them bitches with him; I always end up with tears in my eyes.

"I fucked up. I'm sorry," he says nonchalantly.

I look up at him, amazed yet again. Is he sorry for cheating on me in the first place? Is he saying sorry for all this heartache he, and his bitch, has caused?

"I should have remembered what day it was," he says, and I sigh, defeated. I knew it was too good to be true.

"So, you gone keep fucking them?" I'm tired.

"Divine."

"Woo."

"Shit's not that simple."

"But it is. You know what, Woo; I could stop fucking Gavriil. I could even go to his house and shoot him in the fucking face right now. But you, you can't let that bitch go. That's how loyal I am to yo ass; I could fuck anybody over for you. I'm done now though; Woo, I will never beg for you to get rid of that bitch again. I'm the fool here. I should have beat yo ass that day in the warehouse. I should have never let that hoe into my world." I begin sobbing like a child. I'm so heartbroken.

It's like all the hurt is hitting me at once. Woo would choose her over me. Shit! he has chosen her over me. I've lost; I'm the fucking loser.

"Ma," I hear Milli say. He walks over and helps me out of the kitchen.

We walk into Million's room. He doesn't say anything. The last time I cried like this, Bobby was moving in. The tears I cry because of this hoe. I lie down in Milli's bed, and he gets in too. I just stare at his face; I hope he never treats the girl he loves this way; this is bull shit. I close my eyes and dread waking up. My feelings are hurt.

It took a couple of weeks, but things in the Carver household were finally back to normal. I stopped speaking to Woo. He finally got me to talk to him after the first week by using my precious baby. I could never go against her, and she is always on her daddy's side. Gucci made a nice addition to the family. I decided to keep her with me, fuck Woo. Funny enough, she and Bobby can't seem to get along. It irritates Woo; I think it's hilarious. I enrolled Gucci into school with Milli. He was all too happy to help take care of her. My baby has a crush.

Walking into the kitchen, I smile while saying good morning to everybody. Woo is leaning on the counter while lecturing Milli about something.

"So, when he told you his sob story, what you do?"

Why is he so loud so early?

"I gave him an extra day," Milli answers.

Woo begins shaking his head, "and now what? You can't find his ass, right?" Milli nods his head. "Divine, he gets this sentimental shit from you."

I scrunch my face up, "how I get dragged into this? I just walked in the kitchen," I go take a seat in my nook and observe.

"Milli, take this shit as a lesson. People are fucking trash. Most words mean shit when they come out of a trash can's mouth." I shake my head; I remember getting this same speech a long time ago. "Don't trust nobody in them streets, one slip up and that's yo life. You got it way easier than Divine and I had it. We passing our shit down to you. We had to work for ours. It doesn't matter how you got it, nigga it's yours now. So, are you gone just let him take yo shit?"

"No," Milli answers.

"Then go get it and don't come back unless you got him and yo money with you."

Milli walks out of the house, headed to clean up his fuck up. Woo looks over at me, "So what you got up for today?"

"I found Mook," I say, looking at Bobby. I stand, grabbing an apple off the counter. "Let's go, Gucci."

We walk out of the house. I look over at Gucci; she has her phone out, texting someone *'be safe.'* I begin laughing.

"What so funny?" she asks, smiling.

"Nothing; I can laugh," I say, smiling harder.

They think they are so slick.

"Where we going?" Gucci asks.

"To ask a man if he thinks I'm a joke."

Pulling up to an unfamiliar block, I see Raylo has arrived first. I step out of the car as he walks over to me.

"Why you bring the minor?" he asks, looking at Gucci.

"I turned eighteen last week," she says with an attitude.

"Give her a piece," I say, ignoring both.

"Does she even know how to use it?"

"Million taught me," she answers, taking a gun out of his hand.

"How many people in there?"

"Just Mook and his three cousins."

"I guess he feels safe," I smirk, "send Smoke and Jackson to the back of the house to make sure nobody makes a run for it."

Raylo whistles, then hand signals his men to the back of the house as lookouts. They make their way up the driveway. The young boy that I don't know walks over to us.

"Boss lady, this Sam; Sam, this boss lady," Raylo introduces us.

"Whose house is this?" I ask.

"Mook's. He just put it in his baby momma's name," the boy answers.

I should smack the shit out of Bobby. I walk onto the porch of the house.

"Are we knocking on the door?" Gucci asks, walking behind me with her gun out.

I open the screen door and step to the side, holding it open. Gucci steps to the side, confused as Raylo walks up, kicking the door in. He walks in first, and I follow behind him. We walk into the living room where the three cousins are sitting watching a football game on tv. Raylo and Gucci have their guns pulled and aimed at them. I hear music upstairs. I look at Sam and signal him to go upstairs.

Raylo makes the three stogies sit on the floor with their hands on their heads. I take a seat on the couch. I hear a gunshot go off upstairs; I shake my head. Then I hear a commotion. It's quiet for a bit, and then a gunshot goes off in the backyard. I pull my phone out. We hear the back door open; Mook is walked in by Smoke and Jackson.

"Smoke," I point to the stairs, "go upstairs and see what happened."

Raylo grabs Mook by his shirt and puts him down on his knees in front of me. Smoke comes from upstairs shaking his head. Damn, I just fucking met Sam.

"Hey Mook, how have you been?"

"Look, Divine, I have your money. Just let me go get it."

I look at Raylo, laughing, "he said he has my money. I know you have my money. Why else would I be here?"

"You been hiding from this bitch the whole time?" one of his cousins says, looking at me, "I wish you would have told me; I would have put her in check for you."

"You don't check Queens," I say, bored with the situation.

"Bit..." Before he can even finish the word, my gun is out and there's a bullet now in his face.

"Mook, where is my money?" I ask, irritated.

Rattled, "in in the basement," Mook responds.

"Where in the basement?"

"Behind the dryer."

I nod at Jackson. Looks like it's his turn. He begins opening doors looking for the one with stairs.

"Mook, why you put me through all this?"

Jackson walks into the living room with a plastic bag full of money. I look at the bag then back at Mook.

"This isn't nearly enough money, Mook."

Sick of his shit, I shoot his other cousin in the face.

"The dyke bitch took it," his last cousin shouts.

"What's your name?" I ask.

"Deonte."

"Well, Deonte, what dyke bitch are you talking about?"

"He is talking about Bobby," Mook answers for him.

I look at Mook perplexed, "why would Bobby take my money?"

"She told me that she would get my family out of here. I knew you would kill me regardless, so I took her up on her offer."

"Gucci," I call out.

Gucci quickly raises her gun and shoots Mook in the head. I pick the money up and walk out of the door. A waste of fucking time. I walk out of the house pissed. Things were just going back to normal; living in the house was becoming ok again. Now I have to kill her.

"Burn this fucking house down to the fucking ground. I don't want there to be anything left."

I get in my car, Gucci follows. I pick up my phone and call Woo.

"Divine."

"Where are you?"

"Warehouse."

I hang up the phone; I am fucking pissed. I don't know what I'm madder at. This bitch knew where Mook was and that I was looking for him. This bitch took my money from him, leaving me this chump change. Or the fact that this hoe interfered, period. If you ask me, it's all disrespectful. I'm driving like a madwoman trying to get to the damn warehouse. This hoe has become too comfortable. She is about to find out just who the fuck I am.

Pulling into the lot, I come to a screeching stop. I pull my gun out because I'm about to smack the shit out of her ass with it. I walk past the men at the door and the countless men and women counting money, sorting guns, and creating drugs. I have one goal in mind.

Making it to the back of the warehouse, there's a closed-door; I open it. There's Woo and Milli standing over the man I assume tried to get one over on Milli. I look to the right and see my target standing without a care in the world. By now, everyone is looking at me. I walk right over to Bobby and slap her as hard as I can with the butt of my gun.

"That just felt so fucking good," I say.

I kick her right in the fucking stomach. I pull my leg back to kick her again. Before I am able to do that, Woo has his arms around me, pulling me to the other side of the room.

"Divine, what the fuck?" he yells.

I hear a gunshot go off and see that Milli just killed the bloody guy.

"This family business," he says, shrugging.

"Get the fuck off me," I say, pushing Woo away.

"What happen?" he yells in my face.

Taking the same demeanor, I yell back, "why don't you ask that bitch what she did?"

I look over and see Asia helping her up. Woo takes a deep breath and steps back from me.

While he is still looking at me, "Bobby, what did you do?"

She doesn't answer him; she stands there leaning on Asia while holding her head and stomach. I begin pacing, see I'm too fucking nice. If I wasn't so nice to these hoes, they wouldn't always try me. From now on, if I don't like somebody, I'm shooting their ass in the face on the fucking spot. This bitch got me so fucking mad.

"Bobby, where is my fucking money?" I yell, still pacing and not even looking at her.

"Money," I hear Milli say.

"What money, Divine?" Woo asks.

"The money she took from Mook, the money she took to help or save, whatever the fuck with his family. The money he stole from me, my fucking money."

Woo looks over at Bobby, "you found Mook?"

Bobby still doesn't say anything as she looks at the ground. This hoe is so fucking slow. Woo runs his hands over his face.

"How much money was it, Divine?" Woo asks.

I look at him confused, "what?"

"How much?" he yells.

"I don't want your money, Woo. I want that hoe to pay me right now even if it's in blood."

I watch ass Woo balls his fist up. I start laughing; I start laughing hysterically.

"You gone let this hoe get away with disrespecting me?" I ask, not believing my ears.

"Just tell me how much money it was, and I'll give it to you, Divine," he says, trying to placate me.

I'm so lost right now. Why is he so mad at me? What did I do so wrong? It was him that taught me if somebody takes something of yours, you take your shit back. I roll my eyes holding back tears.

"Why would you give me money for her betrayal?" I want to hear him say it out of his fucking mouth.

"Look, Divine, I have made Bobby and Asia my responsibility. So, whatever it is she owes, I'll pay."

"What the fuck am I then? Are you not responsible for me?" The look he's giving me right now, I know he's about to say something I don't want to hear. "You know what, never mind, two hundred and fifty thousand. Mook stole three hundred thousand, and I got fifty thousand in the car."

Fuck this! I'm over all this bull shit. Run me my fucking money.

The Fool

Sitting in the kitchen with my baby, I watch as she eats her breakfast. Vivi is so innocent; all she knows is the love that we give her daily. The life that her father and I had, she'll never know anything like it.

"Mommy, I don't think I like my teacher," she says, looking up at me.

"You don't? What did she do?" I ask playfully, scrunching up my face.

"She says that we are all her favorites, but that's not true."

"Why isn't it true?"

"She only gives Harvey the gold stars."

I try to hold back my smile. Milli walks into the kitchen, grabbing a bowl of cereal. Vivi is still looking at me.

"So, what do you have to do to get these gold stars?"

She sighs loudly, "you have to raise your hand in class, and we have to always be nice to each other."

I look over at Milli smirking, and he shakes his head.

"Are you doing those things?"

Vivi slumps down into her seat. Gucci walks into the kitchen, grabbing a bowl as well.

"Vivi."

"Daddy said I'm his little girl, so I don't have to be nice to everybody." I smile down at her.

"But you want gold stars too, right?"

"Yeah."

"Yes," Milli says with a mouth full of cereal.

"Yes," she answers, correcting herself.

"So, you want gold stars; you know what you have to do to get them. I don't see the issue."

"It's...," she stops. I guess she's finding it hard to explain herself. I wait patiently for her to find her words. Then she sighs, putting her head down. My little baby is stressed.

"Alright, check this out." She looks up at me as I lean over the counter. "Ms. Lily, who you used to like, told you and your classmates that she would give gold stars to the students that are kind and participate in class?"

"Yes."

"And so far, that is what she has been doing? She has been giving the stars out?"

Vivi sighs, "yes."

"Little Rovina hasn't received a gold star?"

"No."

"Because she doesn't think she needs to be nice?" This time she doesn't answer. "Well, it sounds to me like this is a problem that Rovina can solve. Ms. Lily laid the guidelines out; it's now your job to fulfill them. You want a gold star, so do what you have to do to get one. Besides, your father's mind is a bit warped," I say, twirling my finger around my head. She begins laughing.

"Be kind to everyone," Milli adds, getting up to clean his and Gucci's bowls. "Go get your shoes and coat and let's roll." She jumps off her stool and runs up to her room.

"Woo is a fucking fool," I say, staring at the doorway Vivi just ran through.

"Your husband," Milli says, texting on his phone.

"Your husband," I say, mimicking him. "Did Raylo call you last night?"

"Yes, I spoke to him, he thinks we should bring everybody together for a meeting. You know since I got promoted."

Ignoring him, "Are yall going to school?"

"Yes, I'm sure I have a test today," Gucci says. And if she's going, that means Milli is going.

I begin pouting; I'm going to be bored. My kiddies are leaving me.

"I'm jealous. I wish I went to school," I say, walking over to my nook, plopping down.

"Go to school then," Woo says, walking into the kitchen.

The fuck is he talking to me for. After he gave me my money back, I haven't been liking his ass too much. Our relationship worked due to the respect I believed he had for me. That shit has flown out of the fucking window. Woo doesn't care about anybody but his fucking self. I've decided that I'll only care about myself as well. If Woo wants to be disrespectful, then I'll be disrespectful too. Fuck it, we can both be toxic.

Woo picks up the mess Vivi left behind. I look at Milli and watch as he and Gucci flirt with each other. Bobby walks into the kitchen; the titty I put on her head has gone down. I glare as Woo walks over to the Keurig making a cup of coffee; I notice this because he doesn't drink fucking coffee. Once the coffee is finished, he walks the mug over to Bobby.

Over the past couple of days, I've been watching them. The way he takes care of her makes my whole-body burn with anger.

All these years, every chance he got, he threw the fact that I was fucking Gavriil up in my face, yet every morning he walks into this kitchen making this bitch coffee. My mind can't help but compare the way he treats her to the way he treats me. Woo has never treated me gently; he was always tough with me to make me stronger, molding me into what he believed a queen should be at his side. So, as I get all the lectures, all the expectations, this bitch gets cups of coffee. Pulling me out of my wicked thoughts, Vivi jumps into my arms.

"Bye, mommy."

"We are getting the star today, right?" I ask, smiling down at her.

"Yes." She runs over to Woo, kissing him as well.

"Later," Milli says, guiding Vivi into the garage.

"Bye," Gucci adds.

The kids are off to school. I lean back in the nook, slouching; I pull my phone out. Maybe I should go see Gavriil. I look up, and Woo is staring at me.

"Divine, have you eaten?"

I nod. I know I'm being childish, but I don't feel like cooking.

"Do you want me to cook for you?" Woo asks.

I sit up in my seat, the fuck.

"Cook what? Cereal?" I have never in my life seen Woo fry an egg.

"I can handle breakfast, Divine," he sounds frustrated.

I don't respond. So, there is shit that I don't know about my husband. He's been cooking breakfast for this hoe and everything. Calm down, Divine. Woo and I wake up together sometimes, but we hardly ever meet in the kitchen in the morning. We are always busy, he's out, or I'm out. We are running an empire together, not to mention we're both hands on.

Woo pulling a pan out and placing it on the stove pulls me out of my thoughts. I'm trying to rationalize the situation in my mind. Woo and Bobby literally spend all day together, and I'm wrapped up in my own shit all the time, working, Vivi, and then looking for Woo. She is with him all times of the day, learning with him, growing with him. I have never been stuck to him like glue. Even when I was insecure, I still had other shit I would be taking care of. I can't be like her either; I don't want to be.

This is why he won't let this bitch go; they are attached at the fucking hip. Realizing this is doing nothing to help my self-esteem.

"Woo, you have never cooked a meal for me a day in your life," I say, trying to be as cool as possible.

"Yes, I have, Divine. I used to feed you all the time."

"No, Woo, buying fast food for me and actually standing over the stove and cooking for me are two different things." He pauses for a second, thinking, then he goes back to cooking.

"Well, I'll cook for you now." His back is turned to me. I look over at Bobby, and she's looking right at me. I stare at her with an emotionless face.

Why do I always feel like these mothafuckas are playing me? Because they fucking are. I feel myself about to shoot them both in the face.

"I'm good," I say, standing.

"Divine, you haven't been eating much lately," Woo says.

Damn! this man is working hard. Even when taking care of his flock, he still has time to see if I'm eating or not.

"I'll get something while I'm out," I walk out of the kitchen.

Walking into our bedroom, I sit at my vanity, pulling out my phone. I text Gavriil.

"I'm hungry."

Gavriil texts back immediately.

"I can solve this problem."

I smile.

"I'll pick the place. When can we meet?"

Sometimes I think he's staring at his phone, waiting for my texts.

"I've told you my time is yours. I'll clear my whole day for you."

I become excited.

"I'll text you the address as I'm leaving."

I put my phone on the charger, then go into the bathroom and get in the shower. Stepping out of the shower, I wrap a towel around myself. As I walk into my bedroom, I see Woo standing with my phone in his hand.

"You changed your password," he asks, looking up at me.

"Yes," I answer, walking into the closet.

"Why?"

"Because I would like some privacy. I have never gone through your phone."

"Yeah, and that's because you don't give a fuck enough. Plus, I don't have shit to hide."

"I'm not hiding anything, Woo," I sing out.

I don't feel like arguing with him.

"Then why is your passcode no longer Vivi's birthday?"

Drying myself off, I drop my towel and begin moisturizing my body.

"I just told you why. Why are you in my phone anyway?"

"Where you going?"

"To have breakfast," half-truth.

I pull my panties on, then my bra.

"What's the pass code to this damn phone?" he asks, pissed.

I start looking at my clothes, trying to decide what I should wear. I'm not even mad at him right now. To be honest, I'm happy to get out of this house. Woo wants to piss me off and probably make me stay so he can leave me here alone later. But like I said, I do this pimp shit too. I'm not his victim. I made this choice; I agreed to this open shit. So I have to suck it up and deal with it, and Woo's ass does too.

"The passcode is your birthday," I say, unfazed by his anger.

I don't have anything to hide either. If he wants to go through my phone, then so be it. I walk over to the floor-length mirror; I look perfect. I turn, looking at Woo. I'm sure he's scrolling through me and Gavriil's thread. I'm not about to say anything, as I'm tired of repeating myself. I will not let him get to me today.

Like Ms. Lily, I have laid out my guidelines. If he wants me to leave Gavriil alone, he knows what he has to do. I walk back into our bedroom and over to my vanity. I take my bonnet off, then my scarf. My hair falls out of its wrap, and I gently comb it into place. I think I'll let my face breathe today, no make-up. I grab my purse, making sure I have everything I need in it just in case this turns into more than breakfast.

"Woo, what time does my phone say?"

He doesn't answer; he's still going through text messages. I snatch my phone from him.

"I have to go," I say, throwing it in my purse.

"I'll kill you and him," Woo says, causing me to stop at our bedroom door.

"That's fine. I'll make sure you and Bobby follow us to hell," then I walk out.

Walking into the kitchen, I see Asia sitting at the counter, eating. Woo be in this bitch burning. Woo dares to be in my kitchen preparing meals for his hoes. Asia has a plate full of food.

"You are looking good, Divine," she says, looking at me as I walk through.

"Thank you," I say, smiling.

Getting into my car, I pull my phone out. Where do I want to go? I don't really want to be in a fancy place. I need to humanize Gavriil, bring him down a bit. I text him the address to Bob Evan's; I know he's going to be mad. Just thinking about it makes me laugh.

I pull into the parking lot and text Gavriil telling him that I'm here. I look up as a car pulls in beside mine. It's Gavriil, and he has an irritated look on his face. I step out of the car and look around; he steps out of his car too.

"What? No caravan?" I ask, wondering why he's all alone.

"Just me. If I had told those fucks where I was going, they would have tried to find a way for me to have a meeting."

I walk up to him, smiling. He opens his arms, and I walk into them. Boy, did I need a fucking hug?

"Divine, where the fuck do you have me?"

Letting go, I grab his hand and pull him into the restaurant.

"I don't want anything fancy, just plain breakfast."

The waitress shows us to a booth. I slide right in. Gavriil looks at the table, then me; I smile up at him. I knew he would act like this.

"Sit," I say, letting my laughter out.

"This is not funny," he picks up the silverware, inspecting it.

"You need more humble women in your life, Gavi. You are too bougie."

"More women? I only deal with one woman at a time," he says, looking around the place.

He's like a kid finding a new discovery.

"Gavriil, I am not the only woman you sleeping with." I can't be.

"But you are," he says, looking at me now.

This is making me uncomfortable. This is not the first time Gavriil and I have sat down to have a meal. Usually we eat after sex, then I have to leave. We don't meet just to meet like right now. We only have sex. Even when he tries to make things personal, I keep everything at sex. Before I can say anything, the waitress walks over, and we order. I place my head in my hand and start fidgeting with a napkin.

"So sunshine, what's got you down?"

I smile, "life, Gavriil. Like you said, I hold everything in till it's about to spill over, then I call you."

"So here we are," he says, putting his head in his hand, mimicking me. He looks so out of place here. "Go ahead then, spill."

I start laughing, "You are aware that I'm trying to use you for my own selfish reasons?"

The waitress walks over, putting our drinks on the table. She places two straws down as well. I watch as Gavriil looks the cup over, checking for stains.

"It's fine, princess," I say, sipping on my orange juice.

"I'm still upset with you," he says, reminding me of how we left things the last time we met.

"You and I don't meet often, and you expect me to believe you're not fucking anybody else?" I try to change the subject.

He stares at me. I'm sure he knows what I just did.

"I'm a man that devotes himself to the things he wants. I have no interest in women I'm not interested in. I would never invest my time in a woman, just for kicks."

I don't say anything; I don't know what to say to that.

"Divine, the way you and your husband love is not the only way."

"Don't lecture me, Gavriil. I'm fully aware of how my relationship looks to others. But just like it's not their business, it's not yours."

"Like a child, always defensive," he says, smiling.

I feel like he never takes me seriously. The waitress walks over, placing our food in front of us. I smile, thanking her; everything looks good.

"I am not a child," I say to him through gritted teeth.

"Really? Every time we discuss you and your husband, you pull out your claws. You don't want to hear the truth, and it's quite entertaining. I have let you play with me as you like all these years with one goal in mind." He still has that godforsaken smile on his face.

Deciding to just go along with it, I ask, "what goal?"

"You."

I begin eating. It's looking like Woo and Gavriil want to fight me today. How does Woo do it? Dealing with just him and Gavriil is exhausting.

"Do you like the food?" I ask as I watch him eat.

"It will suffice."

"I just don't understand you, Gavriil. I came to you with the perfect set-up. No strings attached. I have been open and honest with you about everything, shit I'm open and honest with both you and Woo." I begin rubbing my head. "You know today I found out that a man I've known for more than half my life can cook. I watched him brew a cup of coffee for someone that wasn't me. It's not even about the coffee, really; it's mostly about the other small things he's done for her that he hasn't for me."

Gavriil's been eating through my little rant. I can't believe I just broke my own rule. I shouldn't be talking to him about Woo.

He looks up at me, "eat." I pick up my fork, pouting then start eating.

"Divine, I'm positive you won't like this, but I'm going to say it anyway. You are not built for the relationship that you and your husband have."

"I'm literally here with you," I say with my mouth full.

Gavriil smiles, handing me a napkin.

"Just because you're competitive doesn't mean you're good at an open relationship. You came to me because you wanted to win."

"Then why do I feel like I'm losing?"

"Have you talked about this with your husband?"

"What are you? My therapist?"

"I'll be whatever you need."

"This is what I mean. Why do you say things like that?"

"Because I am a man Divine, not some little boy. I don't sit around thinking about what I want. I know what I want, and I don't need options when what I want is right in front of me. I will not lie to myself or you. You just met him first. Now have you talked to your husband about this loser shit?"

Well, I've pissed him off.

"Of course, I have. Like you, I also know what I want. I know what I'll stand for and what I won't stand for. Why should I stay at home being the perfect wife as he fucks freely? I'll fuck freely too."

Gavriil begins smirking. "Divine."

The waitress walks over, clearing our plates. Before she walks away, Gavriil asks for a cup of coffee.

"Besides me, how many other people have you slept with?"

"Just one other person."

"Where is he?"

"I don't know, but I told you about him."

"The point is you do not fuck freely."

"I don't want to talk about this," I really don't.

"Why? I think we're having a great conversation."

I glare at Gavriil; he's so damn annoying. I smile to myself.

"You're a hypocrite. You know I'm married and that I love him. Yet you still fuck me. You tell me you love and want me, but you still watch me as I walk away from you. So this situation we have is convenient for you too."

"If I were to take you forcefully right now, would you accept me?" he asks.

"No."

"If I were to kill your annoying childlike husband, would you come to me?"

"No."

"So that leaves me with one other choice. I have lived a life where I don't mind waiting. You see, little girl, your fragile relationship will break; it will crumble. And when it does, you will remember my words. All I have to do is wait, and you will come to me."

I stare at him, soaking up what he just said.

"My loyalty isn't fragile."

"Don't I know it?" he says, standing. He pulls two hundred dollar bills out of his pocket, tossing them on the table. "Come, I have work, and you need to get back to your husband."

I stand, following him out of the door. He walks me to my car; I unlock the doors and he opens my door for me.

"Look, Divine, I want you to be happy," I look up at him, "I'm aware that you don't believe I can give you the happiness you want. Just know, this arrangement we have can only be ended by you. I'll always answer your call. Go home, talk, be happy again."

He leans down, kissing me on my forehead.

"Goodbye, Gavriil."

"Goodbye, Divine."

I watch as he walks to his car and pulls out of the parking lot. I sit there staring at my steering wheel. Talking to him has made me feel a little better. I don't have friends, so talking to someone who knows me always helps. I don't want Gavriil to be right; I don't want my relationship to crumble.

Alright, Woo, you have won yet again; I'll let Gavriil go. I'll be the fucking fool.

Harsh Reality

Pulling into the garage, I see Woo is still home. Maybe Gavriil is right. Maybe I'm not meant to be out here having multiple relationships. I walk into the house; the kitchen's empty. Maybe I should take a nap and sleep on it. Walking into the bedroom, I see Woo is lying in bed, surprising. I was sure he'd been to somewhere with his hoes.

"That was quick," he says, sitting up on the bed.

"I told you it was just breakfast," I say, rolling my eyes.

"From now on, Divine, stop running to him if you have a problem with me."

Stop creating problems, I think to myself.

"Anything I offer you, you take. How you gone tell me you not hungry then go out?"

"Ok, Woo," I say, walking into the closet. I begin undressing. I put on some pajama pants and a t-shirt. Then I walk to my vanity.

"What's wrong with you?" he asks.

I look at him in the reflection of the mirror.

"I'm tired of talking about the same shit. It seems like whenever we're in the same room, you talking about Gavriil, and I'm talking about Bobby. I'm married to you."

He sits there saying nothing. I begin rewrapping my hair.

"Divine."

"Woo, you put that bitch before me. You've never done that before, and it's really fucking with me."

"Divine," he tries cutting me off.

"No, Woo, fuck her. I'm number one. Nobody should ever come before me. Are you acting this way because of Gavriil?"

"I don't know," he answers.

It's like the roles have reversed between us. It used to be Woo leading the conversation and me indecisive. I put my scarf on and then put my bonnet on top. I walk over to my bed lying down. I don't care that it's the middle of the day; I am tired. Woo lays down with me, and we're facing each other. He starts smiling. Looking at his smile, I start smiling too.

"Back when I was sitting on that curb in front of the crack house, I always imagined living a better life. At first, it was Raven and me. I would imagine she got clean. Then I didn't have to take care of her anymore. That dream started changing when some little ashy girl would always run towards me yelling my name."

I smile. I was ashy.

"Fuck you, Woo," I say, laughing.

"I'm serious, Divine. I have never imagined my life being lived with anybody but you. All this shit, all this work we put in, we did this shit together."

"You and me," I add.

"I thought giving you my last name, giving you everything I have, would be enough."

"How could that have been enough when I didn't want any of that in the first place? The only thing I ever wanted was for me to be yours and you to be mine. Everything I know about the world, I learned for you. Every happy memory I have about anything, you're there. I'm so hurt because you are my everything."

"Divine, you're everything to me too."

"No, I'm not. If I was everything to you, I would be enough. You wouldn't need a Bobby. I came to terms with this long ago because you promised me that I was your wife, and I would always be number one."

"That's what I'm saying. Divine, do you think I go through Bobby's phone? Or notice that she hasn't eaten because she's stressed. You compare yourself with her when I tell you time and time again that you're my queen. In all this bullshit, you are my partner. I couldn't do this shit with anybody else."

"You tell me, sure, but do you show it? My birthday flew by as if it was a regular day. You got mad at me for spending it with Gavriil, but you spent my birthday with her. The way I am today is your doing. There was a time when I would sit in the house, cry, call Bobby's phone, screaming. That Divine is gone. I'll move to whatever beat you play."

We lay in silence; I replay the words he just spoke in my head over and over again. Being like this with him is so nostalgic. Neither of us is angry. We're calm, both trying to get our points across, living in our honesty because no matter what, Woo knows I'll never leave him. There's too much love, too much has happened.

"Divine, I love you."

"And I love you more."

"Why you got to make everything a competition?"

"Because it's true. My love runs so deep I don't understand it." I feel my eyes watering, "I would do anything to make you happy; I have done everything to make you happy. I even told Gavriil goodbye today, like a fool, just to make you happy."

"Why would you be a fool?"

I don't answer. I just close my eyes. Like I said, I'm tired. He pulls me close to him and begins kissing my forehead.

"I'm tired, Woo."

"I know, baby, I'm sorry."

I allow myself to drift off into a deep sleep. Emotions are draining.

"Ma," I hear Milli yell as he walks into my bedroom.

"Yes," I say from my closet as I put my earrings on.

He walks into the closet, "can you tie my tie?"

"Gucci don't know how to tie a bow?" I ask, looking at him through the mirror.

"No, and your husband just left."

Of course, he did. After our little pillow talk a couple of months back, nothing changed. They still parade around as they did before, and I, the fool, only text Gavriil every now and then. I miss him, I didn't think I would, but I do. I've always liked being around him. I look myself over in the mirror.

"Call Gucci in here."

Damn! I look good.

I walk out of my closet and sit at my vanity; I do love looking at myself. I look over my hair and apply some more lipstick.

"Did you remember to take Vivi's bag to Rena's?"

"Yes Ma," he says, sounding irritated.

I smile because I know he doesn't want to go to this party; shit, I don't either.

"They left without us," Gucci says, walking into my bedroom slaying the dress I picked out for her.

"They do that," Milli says, standing.

"Damn! Girl, you look gorgeous," I look her up and down. She twirls around, smiling.

"Come on, boy, do you want to send Gucci by herself looking like that?"

Milli looks at me, not saying anything. That's what I thought. I place the tie around his neck and start explaining to Gucci how to do it. Once I finish, I untie it and hand it to her. Once I look myself and them over one last time, we head for the door. This is going to be fun.

"Why your boyfriend throwing this party anyway?" Milli asks with his eyes on the road.

"Gavriil is not my boyfriend, and to be honest with you, I don't know," I answer.

Milli pulls into the venue, and some men open our doors.

"The bell of the ball." I look up and see Viktor.

"Hi Vik, it's been a while," I say, letting him take my hand kissing it.

"Million," Viktor says, acknowledging him.

"Viktor," Milli says.

"And who might this be?" Viktor says, looking at Gucci.

"My future daughter-in-law," I say, teasing Milli.

We're in public, so he doesn't react the way I want him to; he just continues looking at Viktor. Viktor escorts us into the building, and once we get to the door, he steps to the side. Alright, here I go. It's time to put on a show. Milli and Gucci stand behind me, I do wish Woo would have waited for me, but I'll be fine. If you can't stand alone, then why stand at all? The door opens, and I walk through them; the Queen has fucking arrived.

Walking through the sea of people, they all flock to me, telling me how wonderful I look and how good it is to see me again. It's all fake; it's all trash. Most of the men in this room hate me, either because I won't fuck them or because my empire is standing like a brick wall in their way. Most of the women in this room hate me because I'm married to Woo. That slick fucker has probably charmed the panties off them all.

Speaking of, I look over and see Woo sitting at a table with Bobby and Asia. Making my way over to the table, I realize only two seats are available. I nod for Milli and Gucci to sit. I stare at Woo, wondering whatever he will do. Will he make Bobby get up so I can sit, or will he leave me standing? Woo smirks at me; he knows what I'm thinking. There are many eyes on me; I can feel them. I do love being the center of attention. I walk around the table and take a seat in Woo's lap.

"You didn't wait for me."

"You had you an escort," he says, motioning towards Milli.

I look over at Milli and Gucci. They are both sitting, with straight faces—my little stone-cold killers.

"Milli can't be my escort anymore. He and Gucci are a thing."

"Really?" Woo says, tilting his head to the side.

Big mistake, big fucking mistake. My body goes cold.

"Woo," he looks up at me. "You have a fucking hickey on your neck."

I try to get up, but he holds me down.

"Let me go."

"Calm down, Divine."

Getting control of my heart rate and breathing, I force myself to relax.

"Woo, that hickey was not there when you left the house. How much more of this shit will you throw in my face?" He is so fucking disrespectful.

His grip loosens on me; I guess he's allowing me to stand. I need to get away from him, so I excuse myself from the table. Making my way through the party while having some empty conversations, I find my way to a balcony. Lucky for me, there's no one out here; I can hide away. The cool breeze is comforting. I close my eyes. I begin hearing footsteps behind me; I'm sure it's Woo. He probably has another speech about how much he loves me. I could almost gag.

"I had to throw a party just to see you?"

My eyes pop open, and I turn quickly. Gavriil's aura, I have really missed him.

"Oh, stop it. You did not throw this party for me," I say, smiling.

I'm trying to do my best to hide the effect this man has on my body. I turn away from him, looking out into a grand garden. He walks over, standing next to me.

"I'm heartbroken. Comfort me," he says, looking up at the sky.

"Gavriil, heartbroken impossible."

"Why did you cut me off?"

I look at him, "for mine and my husband's sanity."

Gavriil looks back inside at the party. I do the same. Woo's standing on the dance floor with Asia having a good time; they always do this. I turn back around.

"I can see that," he says, stepping closer.

I feel like fucking crying. Why am I always a pathetic baby bitch in front of him? I close my eye's wishing I could fly away. I feel my hand being grabbed; I look at Gavriil with wide eyes. He pulls me, and my eyes go straight to Woo. He's not thinking about me as I follow Gavriil. We go around the balcony to another entrance and down a hall. I don't know where he's pulling me to. We stop at a door; he looks back at me, smiling. What is he up to? Walking through the door, I giggle.

"Gavriil, why did you bring me to a closet? Is this revenge for the breakfast that one time?"

He doesn't answer as he stares at me. Come on, Gavriil, don't do that. Grabbing me by my neck, he pushes me up against the door hard. This is new; my lips part in anticipation for what's to come. His eyes haven't left mine. His lips crash into mine roughly. I wonder what's the rush as he attempts to devour me. His hands move down to my waist as he pulls my dress up. My body yearns for his touch.

My hands move to his belt buckle; I want him as close to me as possible. We both begin laughing at ourselves; we must look like horny teenagers. His pants and my panties fall to the floor at the same time. I throw my arms around him, jumping. He catches me then pushes me back into the door. Gavriil finds his way inside of me like old times, and the sensation nearly kills me. How could I have let this feeling go?

His lips are all over me as his hands are holding my legs in place around his waist. His rhythm is so perfect that I can't help the squeals coming from my mouth. I knew it was possible, but I never thought he'd fuck me like this. This isn't that love-making we usually do. This is barbaric, two people whose bodies missed each other reacting. He puts his hand over my mouth without missing a beat. I must have gotten loud; I can't hear a thing, though. My eyes are closed tight as I'm focused on the repeated bliss I feel every time he thrusts into me. I can't let this go not again. Gavriil makes everything go away; he washes away all the unhappiness.

Gathering myself, I look at Gavriil as we both try to catch our breath. I pick my clutch up, heading out of the small, wonderful closet. As I walk out, I almost bump into Viktor. He has a stupid smile on his face. Gavriil walks out behind me.

"I take it throwing this party was worth it," Viktor says to Gavriil.

I walk away, smiling. I need to find the restroom. As I'm walking down the hall, my phone goes off. It's Gucci; I text her telling her to meet me in the restroom. I cannot go back into that party looking like I just got fucked. I also need to pee and clean myself up. Finally finding it, I walk in, and luckily it's empty. Squatting over the toilet, I hear Gucci walk in, calling my name.

"I'm in here. Give me a minute."

"Your husband's looking for you."

I roll my eyes. Once I'm done gathering myself, I flush the toilet and walk out of the stall.

"Uwe," Gucci says, looking me over.

Ignoring her, I wash my hands then begin fixing my makeup and hair. I spray my perfume on, and just as I'm reapplying my lipstick, some ladies walk in. Gucci's in the mirror looking at herself. I recognize who the women are, so I smile at them. They all roll their eyes. I begin giggling, and Gucci looks at me like I'm crazy. I'm in such a good mood.

Putting my things away, I begin walking out.

"I don't know what Gavriil sees in her," Gwen says, looking at me through the mirror.

Now if I remember correctly, Gavriil did say I was the only woman he's messing around with, so that would mean she's talking about me.

"What was that?" I ask, waiting for a response.

Her friend attempts to come to her rescue, "nothing, Divine. She's just a bit tipsy."

"No, I'm not. I said your nothing but a whore. What would Woo say if I told him I saw you coming out of Gavriil's hotel room that time?"

Getting this over with as quickly as possible, I punch Gwen right in her fucking face.

"Shit," Gucci says.

I walk out of the restroom. Who was she calling a whore? I have enough bitches disrespecting me in my face. I don't need any extra. As we walk back into the party, I see Woo at the bar. I walk over to him, snaking my arms around his waist.

"You not mad anymore?" he asks, taking a sip from his drink.

"Nope," I look over and see Gwen along with her holla back girls coming back in; I smile.

"Did you do that?" Woo asks, smiling.

"Yap," I answer, proud.

My phone begins ringing. Pulling it out, I look down at it; it's an unknown number.

Pulling up to the blocked-off street in the once quiet middle-class neighborhood, I can't hear a thing. The world around me has stopped moving. Everything around me is chaos. Woo jumps out of the car before it can even make a complete stop. I watch as he runs towards the flashing lights. I step out as well, only that I take my time. It's been a long time since I've felt like this; I am terrified, so terrified.

Somebody touched my baby; somebody killed my baby. Somebody cut my precious child's body into pieces. Somebody has taken the only good thing about me away. I thought the phone call was fake. I thought someone was playing on my phone. Then Milli ran up to me with tears almost falling out of his eyes. Woo had to pick me up and carry me out of the venue. I couldn't move; my legs were stuck.

I watch as my baby's body is pulled out of the house in a body bag. I watch as Woo walks over to the officers carrying the bag. He snatches it from them, setting it down on the ground gently. With tears falling from his eyes, he pulls the bag's zipper back, letting me know without a doubt, my child is gone. Woo's flock runs over to him, holding him in their arms as they all cry. I turn my head to the right and watch as my son breaks down, falling to the ground with crying Gucci holding him in her arms.

All I can do is watch; my chest is beginning to hurt. This is too much; I have never in my life felt anything like this before. I lean over, throwing up; I'm sick. I want to cry, but right now is not the time. I need to get it together; I need to calm down. Divine, who did this to us? Who took our joy? How did I let this happen? This is my fucking fault; how could I not have kept her safe?

I walk over to one of the officers that's keeping everyone back.

"Where's the woman that was supposed to be watching my child?"

The officer looks at me with eyes full of pity; he's been crying, "she was taken in for question."

I walk away from him and back to the car. I want to break down. I want to scream and ask the world why this is happening to me. But I can't. Rena has two children, a boy and a girl; they're safe. Rena is also alive and safe, so this means my child was targeted. Grabbing my phone and scrolling through my contacts, I find the name that I'm looking for. I dial.

"Hello," he answers on the first ring.

"It's me," I say, then pause. It's hard for me to sound normal. "I just need 30 seconds."

"She's hysterical; we can't even get anything out of her," the person on the other line says, knowing my voice.

"Just give her the phone, please."

I lean my head down on the car, then begin banging my head on it. I need to feel something, anything else besides this pain.

I hear a door open and slam shut. I hear some mumbling; then I hear someone breathing hard into the phone.

"Rena," I call out.

"Yes," she manages to get out through her sobbing.

"Give me something."

"They were speaking Spanish and...," she pauses, choking.

"Focus," I nearly shout.

"And one of them had an eagle tattoo on his wrist. I couldn't see faces; they were wearing a mask."

I hang up the phone. I begin hitting my head even harder. This was literally my fault; I should have just shot him. I should not have underestimated him. Why did I forget he was a problem? Why did my baby have to pay for my foolishness? I knew this wasn't over, but I never thought, I never even fathomed that he'd get me back like this. No, this is not the time to cry. I don't even have time to mourn. My baby deserved better. I feel a hand grab my forehead, stopping me from banging it. I look up; it's Woo. I'm losing my mind.

Sticking to Plans

The migraines that I have daily have become a welcomed pain. They keep me awake; they keep me alert. I'm scared to fall asleep then wake up and not have my baby over me, shaking me awake to fix her breakfast and make plans for her day. What am I if not Rovina's mother? Who could I possibly wish to be? I wished for this child since I was a teenager, her name scribbled on many notebooks. I knew that if I ever got pregnant, it would be a little girl. I knew that she would mean everything to Woo and me. The perfect mixture of the two of us, my own perfect little best friend.

Like Woo, she was manipulative and slick; like me, she was smart and beautiful. She was such a fast learner; show her something once, and she knew how to do it. She could always tell the mood of the room, knowing mine and her father's temper. She could easily get us rid of our anger. My small, understanding child kept us from killing each other most of the time. She was a thinker; like me, she thought of her words before she would say them. She was supposed to grow up, giving us a hard time as a teenager. Woo and I had already begun practicing our many speeches. We knew what we would say the first time she snuck out, the first boy she liked, the first car she crashed. We were ready. Woo and I were prepared for everything when it came to Rovina. Everything except this.

I've been trying to grasp the notion that just maybe this isn't my fault, even if I know for a fact that it is. Killing a child is one thing but deciding that her death isn't enough is another thing. Emilio had done exactly what he set out to do. I am a broken mess, just scattered pieces of who I once was. It's been a month since I watched the small casket holding my baby girl slowly fall into the ground. I still hadn't shed a tear; I still hadn't broken down yet. I needed to focus, get things in order. Woo tried daily to get me to talk about her, say her name, but I couldn't.

How could I speak my baby's name when the people that did this to her still walked the earth? They could go home, be with the people they loved while smiling, eating, shitting, and fucking. I may have become broken, but I have not been defeated. The news ran the story of what happened to my baby for weeks; it was gruesome. Emilio had shown the world what he was capable of. He'd shown the world that Woo and Divine Carver are human too. He would have been a suspect, but I knew it was him after my call with Rena. I knew that he himself was in that house, all because of that stupid eagle he has on his arm.

Once Rena was released and let out of police custody, she was killed walking out of the building. Nice try, but I had already gotten what I needed from her. Her children are now in the care of her mother; Woo and I gave her money and told her to reach out to us whenever she needed to. I'm sure Emilio thought his dumb-ass plan was full proof. I'm sure he thought he'd gotten over on us. That he's shown us that he was a person not to be fucked with. Little did he know.

Movement happening behind me pulls me out of my depressing thoughts. I look at Woo in the reflection of my vanity mirror; he's staring at me. We haven't said much to each other. All we've done is plan and prepare. I don't know what to say. I know exactly what he's going through. I know for a fact that there are no words that could make this pain feel better. So, I say nothing; I keep myself focused on my revenge.

Today is the day of our revenge. We are going to put on a show. I look back at myself in the mirror and begin applying my black lipstick. Rovina loved it when I wore black lipstick. She said I looked prettiest in dark make-up.

I stand, straightening out my dress. I walk over to Woo, holding out my hand. Taking my hand, he stands as well. Then we walk out of our bedroom door. The house is quiet; there's no life in it. Everything in this big for nothing house seems dead. Walking down the stairs, I see Bobby and Asia waiting at the door. Bobby opens the door, and I walk through it. Getting into the car, I look out of the window and pull my phone out, texting Milli.

"Are you ready?"

"I am."

He replies. Then, I text Raylo.

"Are you good?"

"We good, boss lady, the connection is perfect. Everything will run smoothly."

This is why I keep Raylo so close. I love his absolutes.

I look at Woo, whose eyes happen to be on me. I'm sure it's because the baby he helped me create looked so much like me. I smile, even though it's something I haven't done in a while. I lift my hand, caressing his face. Woo grabs my hand, kissing it. I look to the front of the car; Bobby is driving as Asia sits in the passenger seat, working on her equipment. Today is going to be a better day.

Pulling into the familiar parking lot, with all the expensive cars, I smirk. I'm happy that everyone could make it. This is going to be the liveliest Group meeting yet. My car door opens, Woo holds his hand out for me to take, I take it. Stepping out, I feel a cool breeze; I close my eyes, enjoying it. I have to keep it together.

"You ready, baby?" I say, smiling at Woo.

Looking at me, he can't help but smile himself. We need to smile, even if it's for a second.

Slim, Woo's right-hand man, walks over to us, "we're ready when you are."

"And so, the performance begins," I say, walking into the building.

Woo and I walk through hand in hand. There are at least 20 men behind us, guards from the many organizations fill the place, our men know to shoot to kill, fuck everybody who interferes. Making our way to the double doors, Bobby steps up to open them. The men in the room having a meeting have no idea what's happening on my side of the doors. I look back and notice that not all the men put up a fight; most realized what was happening and stood down.

Walking into the meeting, all eyes are on us. I begin searching for the pair I hope to see; there they are.

"Woo, Divine, welcome," Gavriil says.

I hear Gavriil, but I ignore him. My eyes are locked on my target. Woo helps me over to our seats, only this time he places me in his lap. I don't mind; my mind is on other things.

"Why are there men with guns?" Roscoe asks, looking at Gavriil.

Gavriil sits back in his seat, not saying a word. In fact, everyone sits back, except one person. His eyes have been locked on mine as well. I feel all my words caught in my throat. I had a speech ready, but the words won't come. Why do I have to become emotional right now? I can't lose my shit right now, not at this moment. I feel Woo's lips on my cheek. I look at him, taking a deep breath. Standing, I motion for Asia to begin her setup. Some of our men bring in a huge flat screen tv, plugging it in. I look at all the men sitting around the table. I'm gaining my confidence back, thank you, Woo.

I begin smiling, "Hello, boys."

"Divine, what the fuck is going on?" Roscoe asks, speaking out of turn yet again.

"Can't you tell?" I motion around the room, "I'm getting ready for a presentation." I place my hand on my hip as I begin pacing in front of them. "Relax, guys, it's so tense in here. Should I do a striptease to lighten the mood?"

No one says anything. Some even look away from me. Gavriil's the only one at the table with a smile on his face.

"We're ready," Asia says.

"The connection?" I ask.

"Strong," she answers.

I love Raylo; he needs a raise.

"Alright," I stop pacing and lean on the table a bit, "let's get this party started. I don't know if you guys are aware of this, but Woo and I recently had a death in the family." The room's quiet. "This death isn't one of those things that we can let go with just a discussion, right baby?"

"Right," Woo says.

"So, Woo and I have decided to end our," I begin snapping my fingers, "what do you call it?"

"Relationship," Asia shouts, trying to guess.

"No," I answer, still trying to think.

"Association," Bobby answers.

I look at her smiling, "you know what, yes Bobby, let's go with that. Anyway, Woo and I would like to end our association with the Group."

I avoid Gavriil's eyes.

"Divine," Gavriil finally decides to speak, "what exactly is this about?"

Always going the diplomatic route. He knows what the fuck is up. All the men in this room know why I'm here.

"Someone at this table killed my child. Someone at this table cut limbs from her body. Someone at this table is about to feel what I'm feeling right now." I've always been direct with my words.

Emilio attempts to stand to his feet, but as always, he's slow and dumb. Slim has a gun right on his head.

"Deja vu," I say smiling, "only this time I won't allow you to live." Slim pushes him back into his sit turning him towards the tv.

We all look at the screen as we hear Gucci's voice coming through.

"Did you turn this shit on properly?" she says with a black mask over her head.

"It's on; we can see and hear you. How about you show us what you got there?" I say excitedly.

She backs away from the camera, revealing at least 30 people tied tightly together. Men, women, and children, I've gathered them all. This is the immediate family Emilio has here in the states. I've sent men to Mexico; I will wipe out his whole bloodline. As we speak, multiple hits are happening. It took a whole month, but my plan is finally being executed perfectly. I want blood, all of it. Emilio stands again. This time I put my hand up, Slim backs off. I let him get closer to the tv. I want him to see what I've done. I want him to know that there is nothing he can do to stop what he's about to watch.

"Perra que has hecho?" Emilio seethes.

"English," I say, rolling my eyes, becoming annoyed. "You brought this on yourself. I mean, who involves children?" I begin shaking my head, "you know what, don't answer that. This is my fault. I underestimated you."

A firing squad walks in front of the tied-up family.

"I'll never underestimate anyone again. This tit for tat shit is going to end. I'm ending it. I'm going to end your whole bloodline. Everyone related to you has to die."

Emilio's phone begins ringing. "Answer it," I shout, causing him to jump.

Slim takes the phone from his pocket. He puts it on speaker, placing it on the table.

"Papa," a young voice comes through the phone.

In my planning, I came across Emilio's secret family that he's been hiding away in Mexico. A creep like him would have two separate families. Before Emilio can say anything, gunshots can be heard coming from the phone.

"I must admit, you sure did hire a lot of security for your family, but it wasn't enough." I see tears coming out of Emilio's eyes, "what's wrong, Emilio? Are you sad?"

Roscoe stands, "I can't watch this. It's a massacre."

Before I can speak, "sit the fuck down. Everybody will watch, everybody," Woo shouts with his gun pointed at Roscoe.

I wonder why Roscoe has so much to say. Everyone else is just sitting quietly, letting it happen; they understand. Emilio took shit way too fucking far, so now I have to take it farther.

"Kill them," I say to the tv.

The scene on tv isn't pretty. The firing squad was informed to shoot until I said stop. I don't know what kind of guns they're using, but some of the bodies begin folding in half. Bullets are going through them, sawing their bodies in half. Blood and guts are all over the place. Even when the family becomes a pile of pieces on the floor, the firing squad continues to shoot. I never say for them to stop. In fact, the sound of the guns becomes soothing. After a while, Milli picks the camera up, showing us the damage. I hear gasps and sounds of disgust; it is gruesome. I look over and notice that Emilio has passed out.

"Wake him up," I say to Bobby. She smacks him awake. "Who said you could pass out, bitch?" I ask, annoyed at his nerve.

Asia and our men begin packing up; the presentation is over. Now we get to take Emilio home and have even more fun. I'm still not satisfied. The men begin speaking amongst themselves as my eyes find Gavriil's. I hadn't seen him since the night I got the worst phone call of my life. Just from the look in his eyes, I can tell he wants nothing more than to hug me. To be honest, I wouldn't mind being hugged by him right now. I've been wishing I could be near him.

Leaving the Group was a hard decision to make, but it needed to be made. Woo and I don't play well with others anyway, mostly Woo. Out of respect for Gavriil, I decided not to kill Emilio here. Once we get Emilio to the house, his torture will be long and satisfying. Even if we're no longer in business with the Group, I would still like for things to be peaceful between us. I smile at Gavriil; it's not big or bright. I just want him to know that I'm going to be ok. I feel someone glaring at me, so I turn to see Woo staring straight through me.

Woo stands from his seat, walking over to me. He kisses my lips softly. Then he looks over at Gavriil, smirking. I watch him nervously. What is he planning? He walks over to Emilio putting his gun to his head. This wasn't the plan, I think to myself, yet I don't move or say a word. I look at Gavriil, who's glaring at Woo. Woo's glaring right back at him. A single gunshot, just one. Of the many we've heard today, it only took this one to make us enemy number one. Woo had broken the one rule Gavriil had, and he did it while looking right at him.

I don't take my eyes off Gavriil. I watch as his whole face turns red. Gavriil is fucking pissed. Viktor, who's been standing behind Gavriil this whole time, steps up, putting his hand on Gavriil's shoulder. Gavriil looks at me as Woo pulls me out of the door. This is it; this is our real goodbye. Now, if I ever see Gavriil again, one of us will have to die. The Group had one rule, no bloodshed at the meeting. We could do whatever we wanted outside the meeting. Getting into the car, I close my eyes. Why did Woo do that? That shit was not a part of the plan.

Back to Business

Looking at myself in my bathroom mirror, I'm starting to look like myself again. It's been six months since Woo killed Emilio, and lots of things have changed. I finally broke down; I just couldn't hold it in anymore. My baby is gone. Even after killing Emilio's whole family, it still hurt. Her precious smiles and raspy voice were things I'd never get to see or hear again. When I did finally cry the river I'd been holding in, I was home alone. I'd passed out on her bedroom floor. Milli found me.

Milli carried me to my bedroom, the room I'd been in for the past couple of months. I barely ate anything in the beginning. All I did was sleep and cry. For the first month, Woo slept with me, trying to help, but then he started coming less and less. Milli started picking up his slack. Honestly, Milli's the one that got me eating again. He begged me repeatedly. Looking at his hurt face hurt me more, so I started eating.

I was feeling like myself and was ready to leave this room. According to Gucci, *'shit is mad different,'* her words. Woo got the whole property on lock with security. He's been going to war with everybody, so he felt he needed where he lays his head at safe. Putting on my robe, I walk out of the bedroom. As soon as I open the door, I notice a guard is standing beside it. I look him up and down. I begin making my way to the kitchen, and I feel like I can't walk two feet without running into a man in a suit that I've never seen before.

Walking into the kitchen, I see we have a cook and maids. When the fuck did we get a staff? They all look up at me, smiling. I give them a small smile back. Walking out of the kitchen, I find one of the suited strangers.

"Do you know where Woo is?" I ask.

Looking at me, he begins talking into his earpiece, and I feel myself getting irritated.

"Mam, Mr. Carver is in his office," the stranger answers.

I walk away from him, heading toward our office. It's weird; since we've been living in this huge ass house, we've barely used all the rooms. Things have changed. Making it to the other side of the house, I make my way down the hall where our office is. There are two men standing on either side of the office door. Seeing me, they open the door. Walking in, I see Milli and Gucci sitting on my side of the office. Asia and Bobby are standing behind Woo. There are two men sitting in front of Woo. Noticing me, Woo looks up at me, smiling.

"Divine, perfect timing," he walks over to me giving me a kiss. "This is my partner and beautiful wife Divine, Divine this is Demarco Ricci and his brother Luca."

"I know the Ricci brothers," I say, putting on my fakest smile.

"And we know the beautiful Divine," Demarco says, looking deep into my eyes.

"Well, gentlemen, I believe we are finished. If you have any more questions about my proposition, feel free to call Bobby," Woo says, causing me to look at him.

The Ricci brothers stand leaving, but not without checking me out. Once the door closes, I walk away from Woo, heading over to Milli. I sit next to him, placing my head on his shoulder. Woo walks back to his desk, taking a seat. Doesn't he look like a big man?

"The fuck is going on?" I ask.

Woo leans back, smiling. Asia is still standing beside him while Bobby is now behind his chair.

"What the fuck is wrong with them bitches?" I ask, motioning to dumb and dumber. Gucci starts laughing.

"You went into hibernation," Woo says as if that answers anything.

I feel like I'm about to fly across the room and attack his ass. Maybe I need to just ask him direct questions because he thinks I'm stupid.

"Who are all these people in my fucking house, Woo?"

"We needed help. We needed food, and we needed protection. The maids keep the place clean, the cooks feed us, and the guards protect."

"Since when?"

"Since your boyfriend wants war. Since you decided to live in our fucking room."

"I just lost my child, and you shot Emilio at the meeting."

"I lost her too, Divine. I lost my daughter too. Milli lost his fucking sister. So it's not only about you. We all lost her, and fuck Emilio, don't ever say that motherfucker's name around me again."

Ignoring his rant, "how bad is it? Is the Village still standing?"

"Raylo and Milli have been taking care of the Village and all of your other responsibilities. We are good. Them stupid fucks wish I would fall. My empire will always stand tall." I roll my eyes.

"If we're 'good,' why are we at war?" I ask.

Woo doesn't answer. So, I look at Milli.

"We been taking over some new territory," he answers, causing me to take a deep breath.

I look over at Woo in amazement. His ass has been taking all Emilio's old territories; no wonder The Group is at war with us.

"Woo, this is not the way to go about things."

"Well, yo ass was sleep."

I stand, "check this out, that's the last comment I'm allowing you to make about what the fuck I been doing. I lost my fucking daughter, and I also lost the chance to kill the person responsible for it, so fuck you very much. If your egotistical ass wanted his territories, we could have gone about it another way. And get rid of all these strangers in my fucking house, Woo. I'm dead fucking serious. Also, why are you doing business with the Ricci brothers? It's like you asking for trouble. You know the relationship they have with Gavriil."

"Of course, I know, and I don't give a fuck. This is business. We not a part of that bullshit anymore."

"You not making sense. Why would you deal with them? Why do you always have to go the harder route?"

"Because, Divine, I'm me, baby. I'm king; I do what the fuck I want." Woo stands and walks over to me; he seems taller. "Divine, you are my queen." I look over at Milli, but Woo turns my head so that I'm facing him again. "You worried about other motherfuckers that don't even matter. I'm all you need to see. Everybody stays. You don't need to lift a finger. This is my home; this is where we rest, so of course, I'm going to keep it safe."

I pull away from him and walk out of the office. Woo is tripping, and my head is starting to hurt. Making it to the other side of the house, I begin walking up the stairs to our bedroom. I'm mad at him for making so many decisions without me, but he's right I wasn't around. Walking past all these people, I pretend I can't see them. As I open my bedroom door, I see two young girls making the bed. I want to scream and shout at them for being in my bedroom, but it's not their fault. This is all Woo's fucking fault.

I walk into my closet looking for something to wear; I need to get out of this house. I hear the bedroom door open and close, then hear him ask the ladies to leave. Now he's standing at the closet entrance watching me.

"Where are you going?"

I don't look his way, "I'm going to see what you've been doing."

"I just told you everything is fine."

"Well, seeing as we have a house full of people that I don't know, I'm finding that hard to believe."

Taking off the pajamas I just put on, I begin getting dressed.

"I know I don't have to warn you, right, Divine?"

Pulling my pants on, I look at Woo as I button them up, "Woo, who you talking to?"

"Divine, Gavriil is the enemy."

"I'm aware. I literally just said I'm going to check on my shit." I walk past him bumping his shoulder; he doesn't move. "Or you don't trust me?"

Woo walks over, taking a seat on the now made-up bed. Not caring how I look too much, I pull my hair back into a ponytail.

"I'm giving you some men to take with you. All that going outside alone shit is over."

Yet again, I want to ask who is he fucking talking to? But I don't say anything; I don't want to argue.

"All this is for you." I roll my eyes, here he goes again. "You know that, right?"

"I don't know anything anymore, Woo. I used to believe that it was you and me against the world, but...," I look down at my hands. Now he stands, walking over to me.

"But," he says, wanting me to finish my sentence.

"But it looks to me like shit has changed. This shit doesn't even feel like my home anymore."

Surprising me, he begins kissing me, long and hard. I know it's to distract me, as it's been so long, and I don't remember the last time Woo and I were intimate like this. I throw my arms around him, pulling him closer; I don't care. I need him right now; I've been needing him.

Pulling into the Village, I look around. Everything's looking great. Stepping out of my car, I hand my keys to the valet. Woo tried to keep me locked in the house, but I managed to get out today. I didn't realize how much my body missed Woo; I didn't leave the room at all yesterday. I walk up to Marcia's desk, smiling. She looks up at me, smiling as well, I can see the sadness in her eyes, but she tries to hide it. I appreciate her effort.

"How have things been?"

"They been going. You know pussy always gone sale." I shake my head because she is right.

The door to Gucci's old apartment opens. My eyes grow big. Why is he here?

"Vik," I say, surprised.

"The goddess herself. My eyes haven't been blessed since your presentation." I look away from him, shaking my head. Then, I turn back towards him as he puts his phone away.

"Hey asshole! did you just take a picture of me?"

I begin walking him out. Viktor shrugs his shoulders, smiling brightly at me. I look at him wanting to ask him a question knowing I can't. We stop at the valet, and he looks at me. I know what he's about to say.

"Should you be at my hoe house?" I ask before he can say anything.

"It's the best in town." The valet pulls up with his car. That was fast.

Viktor walks over to his car, getting in. Before he pulls off, he rolls the passenger window down.

"Divine, he's not alright."

"I'm sure he isn't, you know, with this war going on," I say, knowing that's not what he meant.

Viktor smiles, "he's acting irrationally because he hasn't seen you in months. Hopefully, this picture can hold him over for a while." With that, he pulls off.

I knew he took my fucking picture. Gavriil will be fine; I don't understand that man. I know he's getting pussy thrown at him left and right. Why would he be still thinking about me, especially with my husband stepping all over his toes at the moment? As I'm walking back into the building, Raylo pulls up.

"Boss lady," he says, hopping out of his car.

"I see you've been taking good care of my things."

"You know how I do. I was made for this," he says, throwing his arm over my shoulder. "I'm surprised Woo ain't put guards on you."

"He did. I just told them that if I see them, I'm killing them." Raylo starts laughing. "I'm surprised he didn't put unnecessary guards around this place."

"He tried. Million had to convince him not to. You know people fearing you a lot more in the streets, so ain't nobody fucking with the Village. Besides, they know I'm here."

"Yeah, ok," I say, smiling.

I feel a bit better being out of the house. Getting back to business isn't as bad as I thought it would be.

Pulling up to the house, I get out of the car, handing my keys over to a guard. The door is opened for me by another guard. As soon as I walk in, there is a maid waiting for me at the door.

"Madam," she says, taking my purse and coat. I eye her suspiciously. I walk over to the shoe rack, take my shoes off, and slip on my comfortable slippers. She bends down, taking my shoes, then disappearing into the house somewhere. This shit is weird.

I walk through the house, looking for familiar faces. I see Milli and Gucci sitting in the living room watching tv.

"I'm a madam now," I say, plopping down beside them.

"Shit's crazy," Milli says. "All these years we been in this big ass house, it's just been us."

"I know. Like all the fucked-up shit we do, nobody ever tried to come up in here. Now, all of a sudden, we need protection." I look over at Gucci, "was my house dirty when you came?"

"No," she answers.

"Exactly. Fuck! Woo mean we needed help. Just lazy."

"Well, you ain't gone do nothing about it, Ma. So just accept it, Madam Divine."

I start patting myself down. "What you looking for?" Gucci asks me.

"Where my damn pistol?"

I'm about to shoot Milli. Upon hearing my question, Milli jumps up from the couch, running away.

"Yeah, that's what I thought," I yell after him.

I watch as a couple of maids walk by us, heading to the front door.

"Where they going?" I say, more to myself.

"All the guards got walkies and earpieces, so every time someone shows up, they are welcomed at the door. Woo got this shit running like he is protecting a treasure," Gucci says, texting on her phone.

Woo walks in with his toys. Bobby sees me then turns, walking in the opposite direction. Fuck is up with that? Asia takes a seat on the couch across from us. Gucci stands, walking out of the room, probably going to Milli.

"Don't leave on my account, little pretty," Asia says after Gucci, but Gucci ignores her.

Woo takes a seat next to me.

"Why'd your dog run away?" I ask.

Woo begins kissing my shoulder, making his way up to my lips. I stop him, by covering my mouth.

"I don't know where you coming from or what you've been doing with your hoes."

"Rude," Asia says, standing and walking out.

Woo takes a deep breath, "Divine, why you gotta ruin the mood?"

"Madam Divine to you," I say, turning away from him.

"That's right. Queen, shit, you deserve nothing but the best. We should have been living like this; we can more than afford it." Woo turns my head, trying to kiss me again.

"No, sir," I say, standing. "Shower, brush your teeth, then come see ya girl," I walk away, looking for Milli.

Walking into Gucci's room, I see her lying across her bed on her phone and Milli sitting on the floor beside the bed.

"So, graduation is coming?" I walk over to her desk, taking a seat.

"Yeah," they both say at the same time. That was dry.

"Are you guys not excited? Have you guys thought about college?"

Milli looks at me, "I'm not going."

This makes me a bit sad. During the six months I spent lying in that bed, I did a lot of thinking. Even though we've both groomed Milli to live this life, I'm sure I don't want him involved anymore. Woo and I didn't have a choice, Woo and I needed to survive. Milli can literally do anything, be anybody.

"About that," they both turn, looking at me, "I'm not sure if I want this life for you. I mean, you're smarter than Woo and me; you can literally do anything."

"I know that, which is why I'm going to protect you for the rest of your life."

"Milli."

"Ma, if I go to college, who's going to be here with you? I know pops love you and all, but he's fucked up. I can't leave you with him alone."

I don't say anything; he's right. No, fuck that.

"Milli, I'm not some damsel. I don't need saving. Don't worry about me, live your life better. Sure, all this is nice, and you will always have a home with me, but..."

"But," he says, sounding just like Woo.

"I don't want to get a phone call one day, with someone telling me that you're no longer here." I feel my eyes beginning to water. "And what about you, Gucci? This is a second chance for you. Like Milli, you're smart; you could be anything in the world. I've given both of you the choice Woo and I didn't have." The room is unbearably quiet. "Look, I won't force college on you two but think about what you could see yourself doing that's not this. This is bullshit; this shit took one of my babies already."

"Alright," Milli says, "I'll think about it. Please don't cry."

"I'll think about it too," Gucci says with a small smile, "nobody's ever told me I could be anything."

I take a deep breath, "I know I'm not your mother, but I didn't take you in so you could live in this life. I wanted to give you a chance. We started off wrong, but we can fix it. Be better than all of us." I wipe my face, "I sound like a hypocrite." They both laugh. "I'm jealous that the two of you even get a graduation, so let me be excited."

"Music," Milli says out loud.

"Music?" I repeat, looking at him confused.

"I want to do music," he says.

"Music it is then," I can't help the bright smile on my face.

Before Rovina's murder, you couldn't tell me that Milli wasn't going to follow in Woo's and my footsteps. If something were to happen to us, he would take over right where we left off. But after that happened to her, it's like none of this shit matters to me anymore. The money, power, it's all bullshit.

Million, I thought about him so much, his future. Today was the first time I had ever asked him what he wanted to do with his life. Like I said, I always assumed he'd be just like us. I don't want this for him, even if he's committed some heinous crimes in the past; that's our fault. Now I want him to make the better choice. It's his life.

"What's going on with Bobby? Why that hoe avoiding me?" Woo thought he distracted me. Nope, I have not forgotten.

I'm awake and out of bed. I'm going to find out what's been going on while I was mourning. Life is going to suck so bad without my little best friend. I don't know how I'm going to do this without her love. But it's back to business for me. It's time I get some shit straight.

Shattered Heart

"So, what do you think?" Demarco asks Woo.

I can't believe he's doing this. Right now, we are in some shitty warehouse. Woo is standing next to me with his arm tightly wrapped around my waist. I roll my eyes; we should not be doing business with these snakes. I look over at Asia; she's standing on the other side of Woo with her gun out. Slim is standing beside me with his out as well. The warehouse is full of armed men from each side. Don't we look like a crew of criminals? Someone call the police, we're all in one place. I hate doing things this way; it's dirty and old-fashioned.

"I think we've got a deal," Woo says, taking a puff of the cigar he's smoking. Since when did he start smoking cigars? This fucking smoke better not get stuck in my hair. And why is Demarco staring at me like I'm a medium-well steak?

"Great, then let's do this," Luca, the younger of the Ricci brothers, adds.

Woo has changed, and I'm not sure if it's in a good way. He's involving me less in the things he has planned. It's almost as if he wants to be at war. How could he not understand that war means dead bodies, dead bodies mean police and police means a stop to everyone's money? Anyway, I don't ask questions anymore; I just don't care as much. I've even cut back Milli's responsibilities, and after threatening Woo's life, he agreed to let Milli live as he wants.

The Carver empire's moneymaker is still the Village. It's the only thing I truly care for. Woo doesn't understand it, and he never will. The way I do business just makes sense, and I hardly ever use violence. Girls have been moving in and out lately. They've been meeting their goals, and this makes me happy. My girls never planned on selling themselves forever, and I'm ok with that. Once they've made enough money, they move on, as they should. Doing things this way also helps me with keeping things fresh and new for my clients.

I feel Woo's hand grab my ass; I should smack the fuck out of him. I know he's doing it because of all the attention Demarco's paying me. Fuck these guns and fuck the Ricci brothers. Why is he treating me like some trophy? Bitch, I'm a queen. He gets the hint from the look I give him. Trying to cool my anger, he kisses me lightly on my forehead. Being around Woo lately has been a chore, like it's work or something. Things didn't use to be like this, and I wonder what's changed.

The ride home is quiet. My phone vibrates, letting me know I have a notification. It's the text I've been waiting for all day. I look over at Woo, smiling.

"Woo."

"Divine."

"It's finally time. We can take care of Korky."

Woo looks over at me, "really now?"

"Yes, he's settled. I'm sure he's become comfortable and complacent."

"Cool, we can send Million and Gucci."

"No," I say, turning my head to look out of the window, "send Asia and Bobby."

"Bobby can't do it," he says, looking away from me as well.

The car becomes quiet and tense. Slim is driving while Asia's in the passenger seat. Neither of them dares say a word. Bobby has been hiding from me and doing a good job at it. I have a suspicion, but I pray to God I'm wrong. I begin shaking my head with my eyes closed. Don't trip, Divine, relax. I have to tell myself this so I don't reach over and slap the fuck out of him.

"Why can't Bobby do it, Woo?"

He doesn't say a word. Okay, motherfucker, act like you don't know who I am. I don't say anything else to him. I got something for every fucking body. This is what happens when you leave a bitch like me without answers. I have an overactive imagination, which is why I always appreciated his honesty. Now they are walking around my house, hiding shit from me.

Pulling up to the house, I jump out of the car before Slim can even put it in the park. Fuck this shit; I pull my gun out cocking it. Walking into the mansion, the maid greets me.

"Madam," she says.

"Fuck all that. Where is Bobby?"

She holds her head down, not answering. See, this is what I'm talking about, all these strangers in my house and none of them answer to me. I walk further into the house; I can't find this bitch anywhere. I walk around the whole house with my gun out; I still can't find her anywhere. Finding a guard, I put my gun to his head.

"Where the fuck is Bobby?"

He begins talking into his earpiece, "she's out-front, Madam."

I begin laughing. I'm gone shoot her just for wasting my fucking time. Milli, hearing crazy laughter, comes out of his bedroom with Gucci behind him.

"Ma, what up?" I ignore him and keep walking.

This is what Woo wants, right? He wants me to care. He wants me to react.

"Oh shit, she got her piece out," I hear Gucci say from behind me.

Making my way back to the front door, I stop. My feet won't move. The sight in front of me can't be real. Woo is helping a very pregnant Bobby into my house. This bitch has been ducking and dodging me, hiding her pregnancy from me. Bobby looks up, noticing me, and stops; Woo looks up at me as well. I feel Milli put his hand on my shoulder.

"Ma," he says before I snatch away from him.

"Shut the fuck up, Milli. I need to think."

I stare at her large protruding stomach. How far along is this bitch? Everything, my whole world, comes crashing down on me at once. Every word this piece of shit said to me was a fucking lie, every word. All this bullshit about wanting to protect Milli and me is bullshit. He's done all this to protect her; he's hired all these people to help her. I knew this shit didn't make sense. Everything in my body begins to vibrate.

Why are they always playing me? Why am I always being played? I point my gun at the bitch's stomach. I don't see them, but I hear guns being pulled and pointed at me. It must be these strangers. They don't know me, and I don't know them, so I don't care that they have guns in their hands pointed at me. But what hurts, what's breaking my heart, the heart that I've just barely put back together, is the gun pointed at me being held by Woo.

"Divine."

"Woo," I say as tears fall down my face, "you think I'm gone let you have a baby with this bitch? This me, Woo. I know you know better. You think I'm gone let you have another family in my house, that I built?"

"Divine," Woo says cocking his gun.

I start laughing. Milli walks from behind me.

"Pop."

"Move out of the way, Million, or get the gun out of her hand."

I begin laughing harder. The disrespect.

"Put those fucking guns away," Woo shouts at the strangers, "this is between my wife and me."

Wife.

"Woo, I'm killing this bitch and that fucking baby, you just gone have to fucking shoot me. Ain't no way I'm letting this shit rock. You should have moved this bitch to the other side of the world."

"Divine."

"Stop saying my motherfucking name. You gone kill me, Woo? Roland, you got your gun pointed at me because of this bitch."

I feel like I'm losing my mind. Everything's scattered, and I can't get my thoughts in order. This can't be real. How am I supposed to react to some shit like this? This fool wants me to allow him to have living proof that he really loves this bitch.

Slim walks up behind Woo, "come on, Woo, put it down."

"Shut the fuck up, Slim. Matter a fact, the next motherfucker that say something getting shot. Now Divine, put your gun down and stop being childish."

"Childish?"

I need to gather some thoughts right quick. I don't put my gun down; I know no matter how much thinking I do, I'm shooting this bitch. Maybe it's not his baby. We haven't confirmed it yet.

"Woo, is that your baby?" I ask stupidly.

Milli looks back at me, confused. I need to hear him say it. I need him to live in this bullshit right here.

"Divine."

I don't say anything as I stare at him, waiting for his answer. Why is he doing this to me?

"Yes," he finally answers.

Woo is really trying to kill me.

"Baby, come on. You know I love you," he says as his gun points right to my fucking head.

I begin shaking my head.

"Don't call me that. You don't love me, Woo. I can't believe I had to let shit get this far. You have never given a fuck about me."

"You know that's not true."

"You love the idea of what you made me. You really think I could live knowing that you and this bitch reproduced?" I start shaking my head again, "I can't let that happen."

"Divine."

Milli pulls his gun out, pointing it at Woo. This makes me cry harder. Woo and I raised him. What is happening to my family?

"Milli," I call out. He doesn't say anything.

"Divine, look at what you doing," Woo shouts getting pissed.

"What I'm doing? You are choosing that bitch over me again. You promised," I start sniffing, "you promised me, Woo."

I can see the guilt flash through his eyes, "that's my seed."

"Exactly, and that's why I gotta get rid of it. It's supposed to be you and me against the world."

I know this man; I know this man better than I know myself. Even if he's changed without me knowing, I still know this man. I know that without a doubt, if I shoot Bobby, Woo will probably kill me. I've seen this look of determination in his eyes many times. It didn't take him long, but he's decided that he would shoot me. The love of my life is going to gun me down. So be it; today is the day I die. I put my finger on the trigger.

Woo speaks, "if you pull that trigger, then I'm going to pull mine. Then Milli is going to shoot me; then all my guards are going to shoot him."

I look at Milli. He has the same look that Woo has. Milli has decided that he will kill the man who raised him if he shoots me. I'm trying to talk myself out of it. I'm trying to lower my arm, but it won't move. I look at Woo as the tears continue to fall. Not her, never her. My mind just won't let it be. If this is how I meet my end, then so be it.

I pull the trigger; Woo drops his gun, pushing Bobby out of the way. The bullet goes into his shoulder. I drop my arm, looking down at them on the floor. Nobody's moved or said a word. I just shot Woo. I shot him because he was trying to save the life of the woman he loves, and she's carrying his child. This realization settles in my mind. Like a virus, it infects the rest of my body. I feel numb.

I feel like I'm about to fall, but Milli catches me in his arms. Why is it always Milli and never Woo? Why was it always Gavriil and never Woo? For me, it's never Woo, a long, long time ago maybe. But right now, for Bobby, it's always Woo. People run to him, helping him apply pressure to his wound. I can't do this anymore; I don't want to do this anymore. Tonight has proven to me what I'd been thinking at the back of my mind for years, since the moment I walked in on them at the warehouse the day I found out I was having Vivi. Woo doesn't love me, not like I love him.

I turn away from them, away from everybody. I begin walking up the stairs.

"I want a divorce, Roland," I say over my shoulder.

I make sure I'm loud, and everybody can hear me. I make my way upstairs to Vivi's room. I go over to her bed, falling on it. I'll never do this again. I'll never allow myself to be played like this, to feel hurt like this. My whole life is a fucking lie, some bullshit ass show directed by a bastard. Woo never loved me, yet I love him so fucking much. I don't even know what is happening right now. How could he do this to me?

What have I done so wrong to him to deserve to be treated like this? I have given him all of me for so fucking long. Why couldn't he love me the way that I love him? After Vivi, how could he think it's ok to have another baby with somebody else? How could he think this shit would be ok? I should just burn this whole fucking house down. Damn us all to hell. I'll never forgive him, and I'll never forget this feeling, this pain that he has inflicted in my soul. If I could, I'd rip my heart out just so I couldn't feel anymore. I bury my face in Vivi's pillows, crying myself to sleep.

I feel myself being picked up. I open my eyes, Milli's carrying me somewhere. I don't even have the strength to say anything. Everything is coming back to me; everything is replaying in my mind like some bad dream. I feel myself being sat down in a car. I look over and see some of my bags packed. The car is on; Milli must have warmed it up. I see Gucci and Milli standing outside, arguing with some of the guards. I roll the window down.

"Sir, we can't let you guys leave. We are under strict orders," suited stranger number one says.

"Fuck your orders, move out the fucking way," Gucci yells.

I watch as Milli gets frustrated; it's only a matter of time before he starts shooting people, as he does not like to argue. He pulls his phone out.

"Tell these motherfuckers to move before I start letting loose."

I guess he called Woo.

"I'm getting ma out of here. No, she not gone talk to you and you know that. Look, pop, I'm about to get in the car and back out of this driveway. I'm hitting and shooting whatever is in my way." Milli hangs up the phone and drags Gucci away from the guards putting her into the car.

Just like he promised, he begins backing out of the driveway; the only thing is, the guards have moved. I see Woo took Milli's threat seriously. I look at my house as we drive away from it. I don't ever want to step foot in there again. It's like a house of horrors. I look down in my lap and notice I've been holding Vivi's red plush bunny that she used to sleep with every night. I sink my face into it and begin crying again.

I don't know how long we've been driving, but the car finally comes to a stop. Milli helps me out of the car; we're at some fancy hotel. I follow Milli inside and up to the top floor. I can't believe this shit is real. I walk over to the window and look out at the beautiful view. I look at my reflection; I have on this stupid dress that Woo wanted me to wear to the meeting with the Ricci brothers. My face and hair are a total mess, and I'm standing here holding a plush bunny. Looking good, Divine, this some queen shit right here. I feel and look so fucking dumb.

"You see, little girl, your fragile relationship will break. It will crumble," Gavriil's words replay in my head repeatedly. He was right, and I hate him for it. Just like he said it would, my relationship broke, and just like he said, I remember his words. Pathetic.

Picking up the Pieces

"Divine, I'm not sure what else we can do. How do you think we should approach this situation?"

I look out of the window of the penthouse. We've been living in the hotel now for three months. Milli packed all my things for me, at least the things he knew I deemed important. Since we got here, I haven't left the hotel; there's nothing outside for me. The handsome man sitting in front of me that's all out of answers is Deshawn Brooks. Milli hired him; he's my lawyer. I filed for divorce two months ago. I just want this to be over with.

The problem is Woo and I built so much together, bought so many properties and businesses. How do we split the empire?

"Give me the papers. I'll go get him to sign them," Milli says, sitting next to me.

"He refuses to sign the papers or discuss anything with you without first talking to Divine," Deshawn says. "Look, to be honest, I don't feel safe going to that property, and if you decide to meet him, Divine, which I do advise, we should do it at my office."

"Things will get really ignorant if the two of them end up in the same room," Milli says.

"Things will move a lot more smoothly. He says he'll sign the papers as long as he gets to speak with her."

"Deshawn, no disrespect, but you don't know pop. And you for sure don't know ma. Bullets will fly no matter where they meet." Milli is so worrisome.

What the fuck is Woo thinking? Why is he refusing to make this easy for me? Does he not understand how hard this is for me? I'm giving up on the only thing I truly know. I turn to look at Deshawn.

"Alright, tell him I'll meet him." I am tired of it all.

"At my office, right?" he asks.

"Wherever. I just want to wake up from this nightmare." I run my hands through my hair.

Deshawn stands, "I'll call you once I set the date up."

I look away from him and back out of the window. As he's walking out, Gucci and Raylo walk in. They both take a seat on the couch.

"What up?" Milli asks Raylo.

"Everything is everything. It's been quiet just like Divine said it would be. Woo never dealt with us at the Village anyway."

"Still stay alert. Pops can flip at any minute; anything could set him off," Milli says, now rubbing his head.

Why are we so stressed? Woo is probably living it up, happy. And here I am, depressed, barely saying anything. I haven't felt the sunlight touch my skin in I don't know how long. They continue talking as I tune them out. When all this is over, I'm getting my son the fuck out of here. I look at Milli. He has so much potential; he could do anything. I smile.

"Woo won't come to the Village. Don't worry, just keep business moving as usual."

Everyone nods their head. I stand, walking into my bedroom; I'm tired. I'll need my strength for this meeting.

"Ma, you sure about this?"

"Milli, I am not afraid of Woo. You shouldn't be either. Relax."

"Gucci, did you hide her piece?" Milli asks Gucci.

"No. You know I'm scared of her ass too."

They need to relax. I got this.

"Milli, I'm cool."

"Yes, ma, I know. That's why I'm worried."

Before I can say anything, Deshawn walks into the conference room. We decided to do the mediating at his office. Woo really scared him. Walking in behind him are Woo and Slim. Woo and I make eye contact immediately. His face is emotionless; I can't tell what he's thinking. I don't want to know what he's thinking. We don't break eye contact as he sits directly across from me. Why does he have to be so fine? I fight the urge to reach my hand across the table and run it through his beard.

"Alright, Deshawn let's get to it," Slim says.

Slim is Woo's lawyer? I don't hide the hurt. Why do I have to pretend to be strong? I'm not. Deshawn places the divorce papers on the table. Slim pulls out a stack of papers as well; it must be all the deeds to the things we own.

"My client and I have discussed how the split should happen," Slim begins.

I block him out. I don't care about any of this shit. Looking into Woo's eyes, I can't help but plead with him. Kill Bobby, fight for me. Tell me you love me. I still love you; the fool in me even misses you. We can make it past this like we've done everything else if you just let me kill her. Please come back to me, tell me you've made a mistake, tell me I'm all you need. I feel like I'm drowning, and I'm holding my hand out, just wishing he'd take it. I just want to breathe.

Tunning back into the conversation, I look away from Woo. I want to say all those things. I want to beg him to choose me. But I refuse to; I'm tired of begging. All these years he spent building me up, placing me on a pedestal. How could he knock me down without a second thought?

"You so mad at me that you forgot how to speak?" Woo says, interrupting the lawyers.

I look at him as he glares at Million.

"Hello pop, how are you?"

The room becomes quiet. Given the situation, this is what he cares about.

"I'm not good, Million. I'm not good at all," Woo looks back at me, "why you letting her do this to us?"

"Pop."

"Why you letting her break our family apart?"

This man's ignorance is amazing.

"Pop, just sign the papers," Milli says.

"You taking her side, damn mommas boy. Why should I let Divine go?"

This causes me to start shaking my head; Woo is insane. Slim tries to start talking to Deshawn again.

"Shut the fuck up, Slim," Woo says. He is so fucking disrespectful; he places both his hands on the table and begins playing with his wedding ring. "You want to divorce me, Divine? You want to leave me?"

I don't answer him. If I open my mouth now, there's no telling what's going to come out. I look over at Deshawn. He needs to continue. I'm beginning to feel small, and I want to be away from him. I refuse to shed any more tears behind him.

"Mr. Carver...," Deshawn tries to speak. His voice is cut off by the sound of Woo's gun hitting the table. All of us are used to Woo's ridiculous behavior, so this display of childish power isn't shocking.

"Divine, I will blow his fucking head off. This mothafucka does not speak for you. Now I just asked your pretty ass a question."

"I knew this shit was a bad idea," I hear Milli say.

Deciding to ask the one question I'd been wanting to ask since he walked his sexy ass in here, I look him dead in his eyes.

"Did Bobby have the baby?"

Woo looks down, taking a deep breath. I'm sure he didn't expect me to ask this. "Yeah, Divine, she had a little girl."

A tear slides down my face, "you let her bring that baby into this world, Woo?"

Woo puts his gun away, I can tell he's thinking hard about the next words that will come out of his mouth, but I won't let them come.

"I'm so fucked up right now, Woo. I can't be in that house. I don't even want to be in the same state with a baby that you had with that bitch." I allow all my fucked-up thoughts to come up to the surface; I'm fucking hurt. "So, you gone replace Vivi and me, Woo? You think that bitch can be me? There is no way in hell that you and I could work Woo, not after a betrayal like this one. You took a bullet for that stupid hoe."

"A bullet that you fucking shot."

"What did you think I was going to do? That's why you tried to hide it from me in the first fucking place. Stop acting like you didn't know that I would react like that. Hiding a pregnant bitch in my house, under my fucking nose."

"We can work through this. You and I can get through anything." Now he's the one pleading with me through his eyes.

"No, we can't. The only way I'll come home is if it's to put a bullet in that bitch and her baby's head." Woo's eyes go dark as he stares at me. I've pissed him right the fuck off, and I don't fucking care. Fuck Bobby and that baby!

"I'll only take the Village." This is over. Woo has dumped me.

"Divin...," Deshawn says, trying to stop me from talking. I put my hand up.

"I never wanted anything from you except love. I've told you this time and time again. All that material shit means nothing to me now. You can have it. Splitting things down the middle will only complicate things. I don't want to have to fuck you up because of your stupid ego. I'll keep the Village because it's mine. You can have all the rest of that shit. Now sign the papers."

"The Village is the most profitable," Slim says.

"What's the Village?" Deshawn asks.

He doesn't know about all the illegal stuff we have going on. Now I pull my gun out placing it on the table. I know for a fact that I'm speaking English.

"Slim, I will murder you," I say seriously while looking him in his eyes. I look over at Woo. "Now I know you didn't think you were going to walk out of here with that?"

Woo continues playing with his wedding band as he stares at me. Like me, he's used to my ridiculousness. The only difference is I'm not bluffing; I will shoot Slim.

"So that's it," Woo says, sounding hurt.

"Woo, you made us this way," I answer, doing my best to not crack.

"Alright, the Village is yours," he says.

Slim does not look pleased, but because he knows that I will shoot him, he keeps his thoughts to himself.

"And Million too," I add.

"Divine."

"Woo."

The tension is once again thick. "I'm taking him with me." Woo closes his eyes, trying to control himself.

Woo looks at Milli, "Million."

I cut him off before he can say something hurtful to my son, "I said I'm taking him with me. Sign the papers Woo, then go make another bastard baby with that slow bitch you got at the house."

Surprising me, Woo smiles while rubbing his chin.

"I remember when I asked you to marry me, remember what I told you?"

I don't answer him.

"It's just a piece of paper, just formalities." He holds his hand out. Slim places a pen in it. "This piece of paper is the same. Divine, you will always belong to me. I'm all up and through your veins. Everything about you is because of me. You think this piece of paper mean anything? Go ahead, go out into the world, see what you find. For you, there will always and forever be me." He signs the divorce papers, "Million you are forever my son. The moment I took you out of that kitchen, you became mine too."

"I'm not the bad guy, baby," he truly believes that. "Divine, this phase you going through is going to pass by like a breeze. My chains will forever be tied around your heart. I put them there; you will always be my queen."

I hate him so fucking much.

"So fucking beautiful," Woo taps Slim's shoulder, "look at my wife, fucking gorgeous when she mad." Woo winks at me, then he and Slim walk out.

I stare at the door that Woo just walked out of. My forever just left; my forever really didn't choose me.

"So now what?" I ask Deshawn as I try to catch the tears that won't stop falling.

"I get all the paperwork in order, then we finalize."

"Alright," I say, standing.

I can still smell his cologne; I need to get out of here.

Sitting on the couch staring out of the window, I sigh. It's over; everything is finally done. I'm free; I can finally run wild. I didn't think I would be this ok, but I'm fine. I feel like I've been having an identity crisis. I don't know who I am anymore, who I'm supposed to be. Woo drilled it in my head for so long that I was his wife, his queen, Vivi's mother. Yet now I'm none of those things. I close my eyes, remembering her face, smiling, crying, laughing, pouting. Her many expressions were so perfect.

"Ma," Milli pulls me out of my thoughts.

I turn, looking at him. He's laying food out on the table. I walk over to him having a seat. I watch him place everything down in front of me.

"Come on, ma, you have to eat."

"I will," I say, giving him a small smile. "Where is Gucci?"

"Pop asked her to take care of something for him."

I take a deep breath, "should we get out of here?"

Milli looks up at me suspiciously, "get out of where?"

"Here. I don't know if you know this, but I'm still a very wealthy woman. We could go anywhere, do anything. We don't have to stay here living in that fucker's shadow. You know I don't do good in the shadows. So, let's go, get out of here. You still want to do music, right?"

I can tell my rambling threw him off a bit.

"Yeah."

"Then let's go do some music. I have a friend down in Houston. We could go and start you a music career."

"Ma, I don't think it's going to be that simple."

"Million Carver, you dare to doubt me?"

"No, I'm just saying."

"I made Woo a kingpin. I can easily make you a music artist. Baby, don't you know, Divine is a kingmaker?" I say, laughing.

I begin eating. I'm getting excited.

"Viktor's been at the Village."

I heard what he said but don't respond. That's another thing I want to get away from.

"Text Gucci, we are leaving first thing in the morning. I'm sure Raylo won't mind taking over for me."

"And your psychotic ex-husband?"

"Has a new family to occupy his mind."

"Alright, what about your mafia boyfriend?"

I glare at Milli, "Gavriil is not my boyfriend."

I don't want to think about anyone but myself. It's about time I put myself first, no more men. All they want to do is control and walk all over me. They all think they know what's best for Divine, but the only one that knows that is me. I haven't spoken to or seen Gavriil in almost a year. I'm sure someone new has piqued his interest. That's what they do. They build you up, make you feel like you can fly, then they knock you down, down deep into the ground. No matter how much of yourself you give, it will never be enough, so why give anything at all?

"I'm excited," I say, smiling.

New Beginning

Wiping the steam off the mirror with my hand, I stare at myself. I pull my hair up, turning my head from side to side. I still got it. I look fucking good. Grabbing a towel, I begin drying myself off. I grab my silk robe that's hanging on the back of the bathroom door and throw it on. Walking out of the bathroom, I step over a pair of pants that was passionately thrown on the floor the night before. Walking into my closet, I lotion my body then put on underwear. Deciding I'm not quite ready to put clothes on, I walk out to my penthouse balcony and look at the view.

Damn, I love a good view. I hear movement behind me; I turn towards the bedroom, leaning on the railing. I watch as a beautiful, chocolate man stands from the bed, stretching. Ben, I believe that was his name. He pulls his underwear on, smiling at me. I'm sure he's enjoying his view. I, of course, smile back; we did have fun last night. Ben walks over to me, going in for a kiss, but I turn my head, allowing him to kiss my cheek. Not so fast little boy.

I run my hand down his perfectly sculpted chest, "you should probably leave. My son will be here any minute."

He steps closer to me, "I don't mind being a stepdad to him," he says, trying to seduce me again.

Unfortunately for him, Divine has a "no look back rule." I no longer ride the same ride twice. He should be thankful I gave him my time once.

I hear Milli calling my name, "Ma."

"Well, loverboy, looks like it's too late."

Stepping away from him, I grab my robe putting it on. I walk into the living room. Milli is standing there fuming. I can literally see the steam coming out of his head. I guess the bodyguards told him about my wild night. Gucci, as always, is right next to him, only now her stomach is doing its best to get away from her; she's eight months pregnant.

"Don't you think you should call first?" I say, plopping down on the couch.

Milli begins looking around at the mess Ben and I created last night when we entered. I don't know what got into me last night; I begin smiling to myself at the memory.

"Somebody here?" he asks as if he's my father.

Gucci rolls her eyes and takes a seat next to me. I kiss her cheek and begin rubbing her belly. Milli pulls his gun out cocking it; here he goes. Just as he's about to enter the bedroom, Ben comes strolling out. Milli points his gun at him.

"Really," Milli says, looking at me.

"What?" I could care less about this situation. "He has a little tech company I'm investing in." I say little, but his company is worth millions.

"Go," Milli says, putting his gun away. Ben almost runs out of the door, scared for his life.

"Always acting like you gone shoot somebody," Gucci says, smacking her lips.

"How long you gone do this, ma?" Milli asks, sitting across from us.

"Milli, worry about yourself. Divine is fine."

"Is she?" he asks sarcastically. "Cause she not acting fine. One of these days, you gone get one of these little boys killed."

"Milli, what do you suppose I do then? Should I sit around, become old, alone and neglected? Milli, I don't know if you're aware, but I look too good to keep this all to myself. Now that would be just selfish."

Milli smacks his lips, then gets in his lecturing stance.

"All I'm saying is, you act like you trying to fuck somebody out your system. It's always somebody different. What are you looking for?"

"Did you finish the song?" I ask, changing the subject.

I'm going to shoot his ass. I'm grown, so I can fuck who I want.

"Yes, that's why we're here so early. He rushed over here so you could hear it," Gucci answers for him.

"So let me hear it," I say, holding my hand out.

"Have you spoken to Raylo? He called while I was at the studio," Milli says, looking away from me.

Now I'm irritated.

"Why would he call you? You don't deal in my business anymore. I believe I told you this, Million."

"He said he tried calling you but couldn't get through. I wonder why."

"Shut the fuck up." I stand and start pacing.

Why do people keep playing with me? I know for a fact I told everybody that Milli was no longer a part of the bullshit. I know for a fact that I told Milli's hardheaded ass to stay out of the bullshit. One fuck up, all it could take is one fuck up, and his career is over. This fool is just like fucking Woo.

"I'm sorry, alright, I'm not like him. It won't happen again."

I look at him, not caring if he heard my thoughts.

"Look, Milli, we have worked hard. You have worked hard. You are on the verge of becoming a super fucking star, do you hear me? And you have a child on the way. I'm not trying to control your life; I just want you safe and successful."

"I know that."

I glare over at Gucci, "why you let him pick up the phone?"

She glares at Milli, "see, I'm fucking you up. I told you she was gone say that."

"Wait, yall coming from the studio?" I ask.

"Yeah," they both answer.

I shake my head, "give me a second."

I walk into my bedroom to start getting dressed. This fool has had the poor girl out all night. Once I'm presentable, I grab my purse and head out of the room.

"Come on, fool, let's get this girl home and in her comfortable bed. I'll listen to the song in the car."

Pulling into the entrance of the gated community, the car becomes surrounded by paparazzi. Million 'Millz' Carver has indeed made a name for himself in the music game. When he told me he wanted to do music, I made shit happen. It didn't matter that I'd never heard him rap before; I knew he would be successful because he had me. Luckily though, I didn't have to do much cause the boy could make a song. Rapping was easy for him; all he did was rap about the life he once lived. Milli is a gangster, so everything the world loves about rap, he is.

Finally making it through the gates, we drive past the different mansions. Pulling up to the one I purchased for Milli and Gucci three years ago—a graduation gift—we all get out. Even though I hated when Woo did it, I have the house protected with security, and they have a staff. Milli is still the son of Divine and Woo Carver, I kept the name, so there's no telling what someone might try. Plus, now he's famous, a whole different kind of monster. For the first year, I worked as his manager, kicking doors in for him. But once we realized that the music industry only wanted to know about the gangster life through music, we thought it best that I would just be a consultant. I made a lot of old white men piss themselves.

Even though I didn't live with them, I still had a room in their mansion. I grab Gucci's purse as Milli helps her out of the car. I am proud of them. Gucci's in her last year of college; she is on the verge of getting her bachelor's in business. I knew all she needed was a little push, and she would take off. Milli is making his legit dreams come true. I can't help but smile at them. Whenever he goes on a tour, he brings home fucking bank. Not to mention all the different merch he's selling.

Watching Woo and me, he learned how to invest his money in different things. Milli owns clothing stores, restaurants and is in talks about owning a hotel. Therefore, Gucci studied business. She can help Milli manage his empire. They are everything Woo and I couldn't be. Walking into the house, I make my way into the kitchen. I tell the chef to get some breakfast ready and have it sent up to their bedroom.

I make my way up to their room. I see Gucci alone trying to take her shoes off.

"Where's Milli?"

"He got a call. I told him to go take it."

I bend down, helping her. Her feet are swollen up balloons.

"You shouldn't let him keep you out like this. You're carrying a baby."

"I'm fine. Besides, I like watching him work."

I smack my lips, "what I say. Now come on and let me help you out these clothes so you can shower. I have the chefs getting your breakfast ready."

"Oh, Divine, how I love thee," she sings out. I begin laughing; I love taking care of my babies.

Once Gucci's finished in the shower, I help her put on some comfy pajamas.

"You always spoiling me," she says with watering eyes.

"Don't start," I say, shaking my head.

"Why couldn't you have found me too?"

This girl is a cry baby.

"I did, Gucci."

"No, I mean like when I was younger..."

I cut her off, "Gucci, I have you now. I wish I had the answers to why bad things happen to us so young, but I don't."

"But you truly did save me. Thank you so much, Divine," she says, wiping her tears. This pregnancy has really brought out the punk in tough-ass Gucci.

"Someone had to," I say, trying to lighten the mood.

"Like Woo saved you?" she says, looking at me.

I avoid looking at her, "yeah, Gucci, like Woo saved me."

"Do you miss him? Whenever Million talks to him, he always asks about you." Then, she giggles, "they end up arguing because Million never tells him anything."

"Tell who what?" Milli asks, walking into the bedroom with a maid behind him.

The maid walks the tray of food over to the table, and I help Gucci make her way over to it. I place another chair in front of her. Milli brings two pillows over so she can elevate her feet.

"Woo's been asking about me?" I ask, giving Milli the side-eye.

Milli smacks his lips, "so."

Woo is a weird subject for us. Even though Milli wants to hate him, he can't, and I don't blame him. Woo was good to him and Vivi. He just treated me like shit towards the end. I'm sure Woo calls Milli daily, always checking up on him.

Changing the subject, "you had a phone call?"

"Yeah, Eddy," his manager, "wanted me to fly to New York for a show. I told his ass no. I'm not doing shit till my son is born, and even then, I might not go anywhere."

I smile. Whenever I'm around them, I do this a lot. Milli has been truly showing me that he knows how to put the woman he loves first. Gucci is always his first thought when it's time for him to decide something. He asks her opinions and listens to her input; I feel like patting myself on the back.

"The album isn't ready yet anyway," Milli continues, "I keep telling his ass to stop chasing bags. I fucking know money. I don't have to do everything for it."

"You're still a new artist, and he needs to make money off you. The gig was probably a lot of money," I try playing devil's advocate.

"I pay his ass just fine. Ma, look around you. You may have bought us the house, but I maintain it. We good over here."

"Well, excuse me," I say, rolling my neck.

"You know I didn't mean it like that. I'm just saying I'm not doing things that I don't want to do. You don't have to worry about me so much. You did good, and I'm a great man."

I look at Gucci, who's been stuffing her face this whole time, "now I'm about to cry." She smiles up at me with stuffed cheeks.

"Call Raylo, ma."

"Oh shit," I say, walking out of their bedroom. I make my way to my room and grab my phone off the charger. Damn, I love these maids.

I dial Raylo's number, he answers on the first ring.

"Boss lady."

"Don't your egg head ass boss lady me. Why the fuck you call Milli?"

"It was urgent; you didn't answer."

"Well, what the fuck is so damn important?"

"It's not something that should be discussed over the phone."

"How long will it take to solve?"

"That depends on how we handle it."

"Fuck," I say, hanging up.

I put the phone back on the charger. I take a seat on the bed and run my hands through my hair. It's been three years since we packed up and left. Raylo has been holding me down all this time; I chose well when I made him my second. I've basically let him expand things the way he sees fit. The only thing he really answers to me on is my Village. My operation may not be as big as Woo's, but I'm nothing to laugh at. I don't understand why Raylo hasn't branched off on his own, but then I remember how my name still rings out in the streets. I may not have been in them in years, but the horror stories still get told.

I'm scared of going back and falling right back into my old self. I love the me I am now; I know who I am, and I'm free to live as I want. I haven't done anything violent in I don't know how long. I haven't spoken or seen Woo since that day at the lawyer's office. To be honest, I haven't thought about him much. I haven't even missed him. But, there has been one person on my mind a lot lately—Gavriil. I guess it's the way things ended between us, and if I let myself think about him too much, I'll end up on a plane running to him.

When I was with him, I truly felt like I could be myself. There was no pressure for me to act or look a certain way. I've been missing his gentleness lately. I don't know maybe it's because I've been watching how gentle Milli is with Gucci, how attentive he is. Sometimes Gucci doesn't even have to ask for something, and Milli is getting it done for her. Those damn kids have given me yet another reason to be jealous of them.

"I don't think you should go back. Raylo's ass can figure it out on his own," Milli says, looking pissed.

"You know Raylo. If it wasn't important, he wouldn't have called me."

"But still," Milli says, as Gucci begins rubbing his back to calm him down.

"Look, it's just a two-day trip. I'll go solve whatever problem there is and be right back," I'm trying to reassure him. "You were the one that told me I didn't need to worry about you anymore."

"This is different, and you know it."

"What's wrong? You don't trust me?"

"No, that's not it. I just need you to always be where I can see you. Plus, I don't trust pop."

I laugh while throwing my head back, "I can handle Woo."

"Let's not forget your mafia boyfriend," Gucci adds.

"Hey," I say, glaring at her. Whose side is she on? "That man is not my boyfriend. I haven't seen or spoken to him in years. Gavriil is not thinking about me. I'm sure he's probably involved with someone else." That last part makes me feel some kind of way.

"And you about him?" Milli asks.

I stand feeling offended. These little shits are forcing me into a corner, and I don't like it.

"Look, I don't like this as much as you guys, but I have to go make sure my Village is ok. Next to you two, it's something I really care about. Now hush and let me pack."

"I thought it was just a two-day trip," Milli says, mocking me.

I begin patting myself down, looking for my gun. He jumps up, running out of my room.

I take a seat in first class and relax. I can't believe I had to threaten both of them this morning; they were doing their best to keep me from leaving. Spoiled ass brats, I start smiling, thinking about them. Two days, it's just two days, Divine. Nobody has to know I was there. I don't have family or friends, so this task should be easy. If I end up having to shoot Woo, I'll be ok with that. He's the damn reason my hearts become so fucking jaded.

Sometimes I feel bad when I kick a one-night stand out or pretend I don't know them when I see them again. But this is necessary; I will not be played again. I'm completely aware of how weak my heart is. I want to be loved while loving someone, but I will never ever again be a fucking fool. I'm just doing what men do all the time. I'm living my best life. I'm still queen; I'm still me. I put my air pods in and turn on some of Milli's new music.

You know what? If by some miracle I do end up seeing Gavriil, I'll just play it cool. I would have to be a fool to believe that he's been waiting for me all this time. If Gavriil really wanted to see me, he would have made it happen. That's just the kind of man he is. Therefore, I gave up on the notion of us ever being together, not to mention the whole shooting at his meeting thing. I'll just go, take care of business, then leave. Easy enough, right?

Home Sweet Home

Stepping out of my uber, I can't help but look around. The Village looks just like I left it, clean and beautiful. I look over at the playground; children are playing and smiling. I see a couple of older people walking around getting their daily exercise. You would never think I was selling pussy out of the building right across from them. I look over to the lot I just bought and see the construction crew has put the fence up. I'm adding two new buildings to my little community. Grabbing my bag, I walk into the building. Walking into the lobby, I see two guards I've never met before. I pull my sunglasses off, looking around the place; I see he's renovated it. It's looking really expensive in here. Classy, damn Raylo! Who knew?

"Where's Raylo?" I ask.

Before they can answer, Raylo steps off the elevator with two men behind him. He looks like a don. If you didn't know it, you'd think he owned the place. When did he start wearing suits? This fool has upgraded.

"Boss lady," he says with the biggest smile on his face.

I give him a fake smile; I'm still fucking pissed. I know one thing, his ass better have a good fucking reason for having me fly out here. The guards that were sitting before are now standing. Raylo really has the power around here. The pettiness in me can't let this be. I mean, I have to pick on him for old times' sake. Looking right into Raylo's eyes, I drop my bag. Before it can hit the ground and without missing a beat, Raylo grabs it.

"Fellas, this is the boss, Divine. Divine, these are some of the fellas," he says, still smiling.

"Why am I here?" I ask, getting straight to the point.

I need to hurry up and get the hell out of here. I can't help this nervousness I feel.

"We can't talk in here. Let's go for a walk." He walks outside, still holding my bag.

Putting my sunglasses back on, I follow him out. He begins walking towards the new construction site. I say nothing and follow quietly behind him. Once we're far enough, he turns, looking at me with scared eyes.

"Ray, what the fuck did you do?" He's making me even more nervous.

"Divine, you know they plan on digging this lot up next week?"

"Ok," I say, shrugging my shoulders.

He looks around, making sure there's no one around, "there are a couple of solved problems buried over there."

"What!" I say, yelling. "Whose solved problems? You know what, never mind."

I can't believe this bullshit. Even when he's not involved, his ass is still involved. Why is Woo still fucking with my business? Why the fuck would he have dead bodies buried in the lot behind my fucking Village? I feel like pulling all the hair out of my scalp.

"Why the fuck would you wait till now to say something?"

"I honestly didn't remember. I called you as soon as I did."

I begin laughing. I have fucking plans, big plans.

"Fuck it. Let them dig that shit up, fuck Woo."

I hope they take his lying, cheating punk ass to prison. I am livid.

"That's the thing, Divine," Raylo says, backing away from me.

"What's the fucking thing, Raylo?" I ask, stepping towards him.

He doesn't answer. I close my eyes, already realizing the answer. I need a grenade launcher and a rocket launcher so I can go blow that fucking mansion up. Fuck Woo so bad right now. You have got to be fucking kidding me.

"Raylo," I say as calmly as I can, "Woo had you put bodies in my backyard?"

"Yeah," he answers, backing away again.

He needs to stay still so I can kick him in his dick.

"Stop walking away from me." I take a couple of deep breaths, "how many belong to Milli?"

"Two."

"Fuck," I say, frustrated.

I need to fucking think; I begin pacing. I need those two buildings to go up no matter what and on time. But I need to get rid of the decomposed bodies that could possibly lead back to my son dug up as well. Fuck fuck fuckity fuck!

"Your brother works for the construction company, right?"

"Yeah, he's a manager. That's why I went with them for the job."

Ok, I can do this, we can do this. I'll never understand why Woo never fucking listened to me. The best way to get rid of a body is acid. We had plenty of it at the warehouse, so I'm not understanding why he buried anything. I'm sure that dumb bitch probably had something to do with it. Looking back, a lot of dumb things Woo did while going against me probably had something to do with her.

"So, look, here's what you do, get our men on your brother's dig-up crew. Have them dump anything they find in acid. Always use acid, always. Make sure you use guys that I know; I don't know any of the new faces. How many bodies are there?"

"You don't want to know."

"It's a fuckin graveyard in my backyard?" I say through gritted teeth. "Do you remember where they are?"

"Yeah, I remember," he says, running his hand over his head.

"Good, you're going to have to be a part of the construction crew too. Make sure you do it at night. I'm sure the tenants will complain about the noise, so compensate them by taking some money off this month's rent. Get rid of the bodies first, then let the construction crew continue as planned."

"Easy enough," he answers, nodding his head.

"Have the acid here at the site. No need to travel with anything."

"Where will we get the acid on short notice?"

I close my eyes taking a deep breath. This day is turning to shit rather quickly. I haven't even been here for an hour yet.

"I'll have to call Woo. This is his fuck up as well."

I begin walking back towards the buildings.

"Where are you staying while you're here?"

"I don't know. I was going to stay at a hotel or something." I turn, facing him, "I'll have the acid delivered behind the fence, so stay by your phone, so you can unlock it for them when they come."

"I will do that, but how do you know Woo's going to help us out?"

I turn around and continue walking, "I don't," I answer.

I hate that I have to call him, but it's such short notice. Looking down at my feet as I walk, I rethink everything over and over. If Raylo does everything as I said, we should be fine. Sure, it's going to cost me a lot of money, but I'd rather pay than jeopardize Milli's future. Woo is so fucking stupid. If I didn't need something from him right now, I'd kill him. I could still just kill him then take what I want.

"How blessed I must be to be able to see the most beautiful Divine?"

I slowly look up after hearing the familiar voice. As soon as I see his face, I can't help but smile. Walking over to him, I give him a hug and kiss on the cheek.

"Viktor, how are you? How have you been?"

He looks me up and down, checking me out, "there haven't been better days than this one, love. How are you?"

"Fan-fucking-tastic," I say, sarcastically. "Which one of the girls are you here to see?" I ask curiously.

"Oh Divine," he reaches into his suit pocket, pulling out his phone. "Our sweet Divine."

"What are you doing, Vik?"

He doesn't answer me. I try to walk away, but he grabs my arm. I look up at him; the look on his face is serious. Since I've known him, Viktor has only ever shown me his smile. Raylo begins walking towards us, but I put my hand up, letting him know to back down. Viktor begins talking in Russian on the phone. Seconds later, he holds his hand out, giving it to me. I look at him with pleading eyes. I really don't want to do this. I know that if I don't take the phone, Viktor will probably throw me over his shoulder, taking me to where he is.

I take the phone, slowly putting it to my ear. "Hello," my voice is a bit shaky.

The line is quiet, he doesn't say anything, but I know he's there.

"Divine." I close my eyes, just hearing his voice is doing something to me.

"That's me," I feel myself wanting to be defiant. I don't want him to know how happy I am, just hearing his voice.

"Have dinner with me."

I smile, looking away from Viktor, "I can't. I have somewhere I have to be tonight."

"Tomorrow night?" he says hurriedly.

"I can't, tomorrow night either. I have a flight to catch in the morning." I now truly need to get out of here as soon as possible. I'm standing here cheesing like a schoolgirl. "Now, can you please tell Viktor to release me? I have many things I need to do."

"Hmm," is all he says.

Just a noise, this kind of disappointed me. We haven't talked in years, and this is how you want to end the conversation with me. I hand the phone back to Viktor; he begins speaking in Russian again. Once he hangs up, he lets my arm go. I punch him right in his stomach; he doubles over.

"Your grip was a bit tight, don't you think, Vik?"

He holds his hands up, surrendering, "sorry, Divine, but you have no idea what we've been going through." Viktor takes my hands, kissing them. He gets back into his car, pulling off.

"That's weird. I thought he was here to buy some pussy," I say out loud.

"I'm sure Gavriil had him coming here waiting for you to show up," Raylo says from beside me.

Looking up at him, "I need your car. I have to do things quickly now. I'm also changing my flight to tonight. I have to get out of here; I have a feeling that Gavriil is going to try to corner me."

Raylo goes into his pocket, handing me his car keys.

"Thanks."

Sitting in this abandoned parking lot waiting for Woo to pull up, I can't help feeling anxious. One thing is for certain, Gavriil can still get it. I don't know why I thought that I'd be able to keep my cool around him after all this time. I can't even handle a phone call. I inhale, then exhale. I look through the rear-view mirror and see my guest has finally arrived. Woo has to be extra; he brought his caravan.

A man I've never seen before steps out of the car and opens the back door for Woo; I roll my eyes. I step out of Raylo's car, letting the cool breeze blow through my hair. Woo steps out looking like something out of a GQ magazine. Why God, like why did you bless this asshole of all people? Did you not know he would be an actual heartbreaker? I sigh in relief, he came alone. I was prepared to shoot both him and Bobby if he brought that hoe.

I begin walking away from the cars over to an open space, away from any possible listening devices.

"Woo."

"Divine," he says, reminding of old times. "It's good to see you. I mean, it's really good." His eyes roam over my face and body.

Yuck, why is he looking at me like that? I should fucking slap him. No, Divine, calm down, focus.

"I'm sure," I say unamused.

"It's like that?" he asks, smiling.

"Just like that."

"Alright, beautiful, how can I help you?"

I look away from him, "I need help cleaning up your mess."

"My mess?"

My eyes quickly find his, "I'm adding two new buildings to the Village. I bought the lot behind it." I dare him to pretend he doesn't know what I'm talking about.

Woo looks at me confused while rubbing his chin. His eyes grow big; I guess realization hit.

"Alright, why you come to me? That's not all on me."

I feel like slapping the shit out of him. I want to ask him why he would put those bodies in my backyard. However, I don't have time for that. I need to hurry and get the fuck out of here, like yesterday. Gavriil really has me shook.

"I need acid."

"By when?"

"Like right now."

Woo's phone starts ringing. I look away, rolling my eyes. I don't have time for this. He looks at it; then he puts it back into his pocket. Some things never fucking change.

"Look, I don't have time for this. Have your people deliver it by tonight. I need two barrels."

"What's the rush?"

"Woo."

"Divine," he licks his lips, "baby, you called me. And while I really did want to see you, why should I just help you? What's in it for me?"

Should I just pull my gun out and shoot him? Yes, Divine, yes you should.

"You think I wanted to call you. I wanted to just let them dig that shit up. But I couldn't, because of Milli. Woo, you so fucking stupid?"

"Watch that shit, Divine."

"No, you fucking watch it, like how did that even make sense? If you want to fuck your shit up, go ahead, but I will not let you get in mine or Milli's way. So have your men deliver the fucking barrels by tonight." His phone begins ringing again. "Answer your damn phone. You are still disrespectful as fuck."

I brush past him, trying to get away from him. Before I can get far, he grabs my arm, the same arm Viktor just had a hold of. I pull my gun out, putting it to his head. His grip loosens, but he doesn't let go. Smirking, he puts his phone to his ear.

"Bobby," he says into his phone.

I yank my arm from him. Woo literally has me fucked up. Like, what is he thinking? I begin making my way back to Raylo's car. I hear Woo snapping his fingers from behind me, then two big mothafuckas step in front of me. I want to scream in frustration, but I turn, looking at him. He is still on the phone, but his eyes are looking straight at me.

"So yall must think that I won't shoot yall?" I ask these bastards.

"No, mam, your reputation proceeds you," one of them says.

"If that's the case, then why the fuck yall still standing here?"

I don't think I can control myself for much longer.

"Divine," Woo says, walking up, "I'll have them deliver the barrels."

"Yeah, you do that," I push past his bodyguards.

Making it over to the car, Woo grabs me, pinning me to it. He buries his face into my neck, kissing me softly. I try pushing him off.

"I have missed you so very fucking much," he whispers.

"I'm sure," I say, finally getting him off me.

"Come have dinner with me?"

Why is everyone trying to feed me?

"Yeah, no. Woo, you have lost your mind. I have a flight to catch."

"Leaving so soon?"

"There's nothing here for me. So I'm going back home tonight."

I'm surprised at how unfazed I am right now. I remember there was a time I would be giggling and giddy in his arms. Now I feel repulsed.

"Can you back up?" He needs to get the fuck on.

"Divine."

I look away from him. Woo gently kisses my cheek.

"Woo, this is not where it's at. Take yo ass home and go kiss on some other bitch. Stop touching me," I push him away completely.

I open the car door getting in. Before I can shut it, Woo grabs the door.

"I know you still love me," he has that smile on his face; I used to get wet looking at this smile.

Facing forward away from him, "Roland, you are fucking delusional."

Woo grabs my face roughly, turning me towards him. Yeah, I'm going to have to kill him. He doesn't say anything; he just looks deep into my eye's. What is he looking for?

"Shits different around here, but I'm still king, baby. I'm still your king," he lets my face go. "Have a safe trip," he closes my door.

I put the car in drive and drive the fuck off. I don't have time for this. It's getting late, and I need to drop Raylo his car and go catch my flight. Pulling out my phone, I dial Milli.

"Hello."

"Millz," I shout, teasing him.

"Yes, mother," he says, teasing me back.

"Yuck, don't say it like that."

"Why? You're about to be a grandmother."

"Lalalalalalala I can't hear you. Lalalalalaa."

We both burst out laughing.

"Change of plans; I'm leaving and coming home tonight."

"Why?" Gucci says in the background.

Why has he got me on speaker?

"I just am. I've been here for too long as it is."

"You saw pop?" Milli asks.

I take a deep breath, "he is such a fucking headache. The man is delusional. I should have shot his ass again."

"If you met him and you both made it out of the situation alive, why you are running home?"

I smack my lips, "I'm not running home."

"It must be her boyfriend," Gucci says, trying to whisper.

"Alright, that's enough." I hang up on them.

I don't have a fucking boyfriend. I'm not scared of Gavriil's ass either. Pulling into the Village, I jump out of the car. Raylo needs to bring his ass and my bag so he can drop me off at the airport. Walking in, I see Marcia at her desk in the lobby. She smiles happily at me.

"Divine," she stands, walking around to hug me.

I accept her hug; I have missed her crazy ass too.

"Girl, you are looking fine as hell."

"You too. How's the baby?"

She ended up pregnant. I'm happy for her and Brandon.

"So freaking cute," I tune her out a bit as she talks. I text Raylo telling him to bring his ass. Tuning right back into the conversation, "he is just so small and perfect."

"They are like that when they're small. Do you have any pictures?"

This question makes her smile brighter. She runs back to her desk, grabbing her phone. I can't help smiling watching her. She runs back to me. Holding her phone out, she begins swiping through the many pictures. Her baby isn't doing anything spectacular, just baby stuff, but she has made sure she caught every moment. I was just like her with Vivi. I feel the sadness coming. Think of something else; come on, quick, Divine.

"Don't you have a plane to catch?" Raylo says, walking up, saving me. He has my bag in his hand, guess I didn't need to pack much.

"Was there a party scheduled?" Marcia asks, looking out to the parking lot.

I'm not turning around, nope. I knew this would fucking happen. The guards stand, I roll my eyes.

"Damn, why is it so many trucks out here?" Marcia asks loudly.

I run my hand through my hair. This cannot be life right now. My mind is not ready for this. Why would a fucking miracle happen? Just why?

Gavriil Ivanov

Going against my better judgement, I step outside. There are multiple black SUVs parked in front of my building. About a dozen men in suits spread out before me, covering the perimeter, each facing away from me. Turning my head facing forward, my eyes settle on Viktor. Viktor's standing behind him, and I refuse to look at him. I was telling the truth when I said I wasn't scared of Gavriil. Why would I be? I am scared though, scared of myself, which is why I wanted to be on a plane as soon as possible.

Just the energy he has coming off him is overwhelming. The power is felt no matter where you stand. I know he's staring at me, taking all of me in. We haven't seen each other in such a long time. I badly want to look him over as well, but I know I'll fall the moment my eyes meet his. Trying to keep my face as straight as possible, I look over to Raylo; he's right beside me. The two guards that were in the lobby are now behind me. I wish I did, but I don't feel safe at all. I know if Gavriil wants, he'll kill them.

"Gentlemen," I say, deciding to break the silence. You would think we were having a standoff. "We didn't expect such a large party. However, we are more than happy to accommodate all of you." I make the mistake of glancing at him; his eyes are narrowed at me. "You're more than welcome to come inside."

No one says a thing, Viktor smiles while looking at me and Gavriil just stares. Deciding to just get the fuck out of here, I take a step towards Raylo's car. Laughter, Gavriil's laughter causes a chill to go down my spine. I don't look up. Why the fuck am I a pussy all of a sudden? Why won't my fucking feet move? Why is he trying to creep me the fuck out?

"Divine," he says, eerie as hell.

I look at him glaring as he glares right back. Why is he mad? I'm the one trying to get away.

"What?" I answer with more attitude than I intended.

With a scary-ass smile on his face, he opens the truck door, "have dinner with me."

I stare at him, "I have..."

"Divine, you seem to be mistaken. I am not asking you."

He leans on the truck. I don't move.

"Do I have to come over there to get you?" Still no response. "Now Divine, that was a question."

"Just dinner," I say, looking away from his gaze.

Gavriil stands off from the car. I walk over to him. Holding his hand out, I take it, he helps me into the back seat. I watch as Viktor walks over to Raylo; Raylo hands him my bag. That bastard was probably in on this. He didn't even put up a fight for me. Gavriil gets in, sitting next to me; he looks pissed.

"This is kidnapping," I say, looking out of the window.

All the guards are getting into the cars.

"No, Divine, this is a date."

This whole car ride has been quiet, neither of us saying a word. To be honest, I don't know what to say to him. I pull my phone out to text the group chat.

"Change of plans," I text.

"Why?" -Milli.

"I've been captured," I text, rolling my eyes.

"By who?" -Gucci.

"Not Woo," I reply.

"Million, you owe me a g. I told you her boyfriend was gone snatch her." -Gucci

I put my phone down after muting the conversation. They get on my nerves. I look over at Gavriil; he's on his phone as well. His hair is a mess on his head, which is weird. Gavriil loves always having things clean and in place. I can tell he's been running his hands through it repeatedly; his suit jacket is opened. He's not wearing a tie, which is also weird. The first three buttons of his shirt are undone; this is Gavriil's way of looking a mess. A sexy fucking mess. I close my legs a bit tighter; it's kind of hot in this car.

I look in the rear-view mirror, catching Viktor, who's driving, looking at me smirking. What is he so happy about? I look out of the window, and I see nothing that looks familiar. In fact, what restaurant is he taking me to? Deciding that this quiet is becoming annoying, I say something.

"Where are you taking me?"

"Dinner."

One word, that's all he says. He didn't even look up from his phone to answer me. I feel myself getting anxious; my knee begins bouncing up and down. I look out of the window again. Feeling Gavriil's hand on my leg, stopping it from bouncing, makes me look at him.

"Relax."

"I wish I could. But you see, I've been kidnapped, and I don't know where I'm being taken."

"You have not been kidnapped. We're going for food. You haven't eaten anything all day." He says, looking back down at his phone, his hand is still on my leg, but now he's gently caressing it.

"Well, where is this food you're taking me to? No, wait, how do you know I haven't eaten all day?"

He doesn't answer.

"Gavriil," I call out, snatching his phone from him.

Looking at it, I see pictures of me and Woo from earlier. Swiping through pictures, I become irritated. Gavriil does nothing to get his phone back. I know how the pictures look, but he must know that it's not what it looks like. No, wait, he doesn't have to know shit. What I do is my business. Why does he even have these?

"You had me followed?"

The car slows down, causing me to look away from him. We've come to a gate; it's huge. The gate opens slowly, the caravan drives through. I don't say another word. I hand

Gavriil his phone back, then sit back in my seat, crossing my arms. In all the years that I've known him, I'd never been to his house. It was always hotels; I didn't want anything between us to be personal. I don't know if I do now. It's dark outside, so I can't truly appreciate his estate. Knowing Gavriil, it's some classy over-the-top shit.

The car comes to a stop. Gavriil steps out of the car and walks around to my side. He opens my door for me, but I don't move.

"Divine, get out, or I'll help you out." He sounds more amused than mad.

I look at him, narrowing my eyes, try me!

Gavriil chuckles then he looks at Viktor. The next thing I know, I'm yanked out of the car and thrown over his shoulder; it happened so quickly that it's taking my mind a bit to register. I don't fight or yell; that would be a waste of energy. Instead, I look around, trying to see what I can, men in suits with guns, lots of them. I shake my head, wasteful. Gavriil walks through his house with me on his shoulder; I'm sure we look insane.

Putting me down, I look around; we're in a huge dining room. It has a huge, long table right in the middle of the room. He pulls a chair out, then pushes me into it.

"I thought you said this was a date?" I ask, looking around.

"It is. I can't take you somewhere public; you'd run."

"At least you know. Why am I at your house, Gavriil?"

"Why not?"

Becoming frustrated, "this is crazy. I have a flight to catch."

"I had that ticket cancelled the moment you switched it, sweetheart."

I look up at Viktor, who's standing behind Gavriil. He needs to talk some sense into his boss.

"Don't look for him to help you," Gavriil says, and I look back at him, "nobody can save you from me."

The maids walk out and start setting food out on the table. I don't touch anything; Gavriil is pissing me off.

"Eat. I know you haven't had anything today."

"Why do you know that?"

"I had Vik follow you."

"That doesn't sound the least bit crazy to you?"

"You refused to have dinner with me. I needed to know why." He begins eating as if this isn't an important conversation to me.

"Gavriil."

"How was it?" he asks.

"How was what?" I ask, confused.

"Meeting your ex-husband."

I stare at him, not knowing what he's thinking. He sounds jealous, but why would he ever be jealous of Woo?

"I needed something from him, so I got it."

"Yes, acid for the bodies. But you know Divine, you could have come to me."

I don't even want to know how he knows so much.

"I didn't want to see you. In fact, I still don't want to see you. I would like to go home, Gavriil. Let me go home."

I'm sure I sound like some spoiled child.

"Well, we can't all have what we want now, can we? I didn't want you to disappear on me, but you did. I don't want you running back into that fucker's arms, but there you were just a couple of hours ago."

"Gavriil, there is nothing going on between Woo and me. Today was the first time I'd seen or spoken to him since the divorce." I feel like I'm about to explode, "why do I have to explain this to you?"

He slams his fist on the table. Out of the corner of my eye, I see the maids jump. "Because you fucking do, Divine. I don't see your face for how long; I don't hear your voice for how long. Then when I finally hear from you, you wish to run."

"I was not trying to run," I lie to myself and him.

Gavriil closes his eyes, calming down. Deciding that I am, in fact, hungry, I begin eating. Why should I starve? Why am I surrounded by crazy motherfuckers? I need to get out of here. I'll just eat dinner with the sexy crazy person then book another flight. Not another word is said. We both sit quietly eating. Occasionally, I glance at the gorgeous psycho, and he's staring at me, watching me eat. I do my best to avoid his eyes; they are intimidating right now.

Once the maids have finished clearing the table, Gavriil pulls me from my chair and into his lap. Viktor and the guards in the room take their leave, leaving just the two of us. I look nowhere but at Gavriil. I feel him place his face into my neck, taking deep breaths. My heart begins beating fast; I need to run.

"Relax," he whispers into my neck. "I have missed you. You could never possibly understand what you have done to me." He lifts his hand up, caressing my face, "my beautiful Divine."

I can literally feel myself wanting to give into this psycho. The walls that used to protect me from falling so deeply for him is no longer there. There is no more *'my husband, Woo;'* right now, there is just Divine. And Divine is weak as fuck for Gavriil. This is why I should not have come. Turning my face to his, his lips lightly brush mine.

"You have hurt me so deeply," he says, looking into my eyes.

"That was never my intention," I say truthfully.

"I told you, I always told you how crazy I am for you."

"They were words, Gavriil. I thought they were just pretty words."

Gavriil stands with me, still in his arms, and I stare into his eyes as he walks. I don't know what to say. From the look on his face, I can tell he's fighting himself. Finally, we walk into a bedroom. Gavriil sits me down on the bed, then walks back towards the door.

"Gavriil, what are you doing?"

He looks at me then smiles, "this is a kidnapping, Divine." With that, he closes the door, locking it from the outside.

Taking my shoes off, I lay back on the bed. I'm exhausted, and meeting both Woo and Gavriil in one day is tiresome. I'll deal with crazy in the morning. Right now, I want to sleep. This bed is comfortable enough. I see the image of Gavriil's sad eyes in my mind. I begin feeling guilt. What if he is in love with me? What if he always has been? I close my eyes, remembering how this all started.

Woo and I had just gotten finished with a gunfight. Black Jackson, a straight-up fucking asshole, had tried to get over on us because he thought we were newbies that didn't know any better. I had come up with a plan to kill him and take over his territory, but Woo thought it better to get close and see what we could learn from him. We learned nothing; the slimy piece of shit tried to make us work for free. So, after his attempt to fuck us over, Woo finally agreed to go with my plan. However, what we didn't know was that the bastard was a part of some shit called The Group.

What can I say? Maybe I didn't do enough research. So, there I was, eight months pregnant, walking out of a gunfight with Woo. We managed to kill Black and all his men; it was literally some shit out of a movie. We were walking out of the warehouse, and there were like ten cars surrounding us. Not to mention like thirty dudes with guns pointed right at us. There were just the four of us, Woo, Raylo, Slim and me. Some guy went to open a car door and out stepped one of the sexiest men I'd ever seen.

I remember very clearly thinking that I would fuck the shit out of him, pregnant and all. His eye's landed on me first. He took all of me in; his eyes even lingered on my pregnant belly for a bit. This did nothing but piss Woo off; I remember him stepping in front of me. I wanted to push him and ask him what about Bobby, but I didn't want to embarrass him.

"Hello, my name is Gavriil Ivanov."

"So?" Woo said, looking the man in his eyes.

Deciding that I didn't really wish to die before meeting my baby, I stepped around Woo,

"Hi, I'm Divine, and this is my husband, Woo. You have to excuse us. We're a bit worked up."

He looked behind me. Raylo had lit the place on fire.

"I can see that. It would seem Black lost to you guys."

"Fucking right he did. What's it to you?" Woo asked, still acting like we weren't outnumbered.

"Truly, it's nothing to me. However, he was one of my people." Gavriil started smiling. Not the sexy smile that I know now, but a creepy murderous one.

Deciding to try and defuse this situation, "well, he came at us first," I said, looking Gavriil in his eyes. Like

Woo, I was not afraid; I just didn't want to be gunned down here.

"Yes, he did, and I told him it was a bad idea." Gavriil started walking around us. Woo went to pull his gun out, but I grabbed his hand, stopping him. "Divine, was it?" he said, stopping next to me.

"That's me," I said, smiling innocently.

"How would the two of you like to take Black's place? Join my Group."

Before Woo could say something stupid, I spoke, "let us discuss it together, then we will get back to you."

Gavriil smiled at me; this time, I smiled back. He winked, walking away, "my people will be in touch."

He and his people got into their cars and drove away.

"What the fuck was that?" Woo said, getting into my face.

Ignoring him, I began thinking. I needed to do some research. How is it that Woo and I never heard of this Group shit? I walked to the car, with Woo following, saying random shit. To this day, I could not tell you what he was fussing about; all I could think about was Gavriil and The Group.

Months passed, I gave birth to Vivi; she was so perfect. I convinced Woo to join The Group, and it's one of the best decisions we've made. One night, Gavriil invited us to a club; he was throwing a party and wanted all his associates there. Woo loved a good party, plus he'd just brought a new girl home, Asia. I guess he wanted to show her off.

I was sitting at the bar when Gavriil walked up to me.

"Mrs. Carver."

I looked up smiling, "Divine. You can just call me Divine."

"Are you enjoying the party? Your husband seems to be...," he said, looking at the dance floor.

I turned my head in the direction he was looking in. There Woo's dumbass was, basically fucking Asia on the dance floor. I was embarrassed, but I refused to show that to a stranger. I put on the sexiest voice I could muster.

"What, you don't think she's beautiful? Wouldn't you fuck her?" I asked, watching the show they were putting on.

His silence caused me to look up at him. He was staring at me.

"Why would I want to fuck her when you're sitting right here in front of me?"

The question caught me off guard.

"You do know I just had that man's baby, right?"

There I was, saying whatever my mind thought.

"Mmmhmm," he said.

I remember wondering why he was staring at me so intensely. I felt like he could see me. Like he could see that I was lying, that I was embarrassed and hurt. Some guy walked over to him. He whispered something in his ear, and then he walked away. Gavriil turned his attention back to me, staring once more.

"Is there something on my face?" I asked confidently.

I refused to look weak. Not in front of this man, never in front of this man.

"I have something I have to attend to. I just wanted to burn your face into my memory."

I looked away, laughing; he was corny. I couldn't believe he'd just said that out loud.

"Don't you think you're coming on a bit too strong?"

He ignored my question and stepped closer. He reached down, taking my phone out of my hand. He held it up so I could unlock it. I unlocked it for him, not understanding why I was so attracted to him. I watched as he put his number in my phone; he saved it under 'Gavriil Ivanov'. He was formal.

"That is my personal number. Whenever you are ready, call me."

"What do you mean when I'm ready? Ready for what?" I asked, confused.

"Ready to be loved properly," he said, walking away.

I watched him walk away. I then looked down at my phone, ready to delete his number. I looked at Woo and Asia, and then I put my phone down. That was the first time I experienced something like that. I was blushing.

You know how they say seeing is believing. Well, for me, that's always been the case. Even if you tell me something is happening, I can easily sike myself out, make myself believe something else. The moment I see it, there's no going back. I could never unsee something. This was the case when I came home late one night. I'd had a long day, and I was tired. I just wanted to curl up under Woo and sleep.

Making my way to our bedroom, I heard sounds, sex sounds. I stopped walking. Everything in my mind was telling me not to look and that I wouldn't be able to actually handle seeing Woo with someone else. But my feet moved on their own; I found myself at Bobby's door. Opening the door, the sight was one that I could never forget. Woo was making passionate love to Bobby; they were so into each other that they didn't hear me open the door.

I stepped back, then headed to our bedroom. I remember feeling hurt, so hurt. Seeing it with my own eyes helped bring me to my reality. Woo was fucking the shit out of Bobby and whoever else he wanted. My husband was fucking other bitches. What was I doing? What was I going to do? Would I sit there and cry? Would I go kill them both? I agreed to the situation; I let it happen. I didn't put up much of a fight when he said she was moving in. I did this.

I went to sleep that night crying hard and thinking harder. I concluded that if I was going to fuck somebody, they would be better than Woo. Why would I go backward? Woo was power-hungry, so it would have to be someone with more power, someone that would piss him off. I got choices too, bitch. I was bitter, and how was I supposed to know what my decision back then would mean now?

That next morning, I woke up alone. The house was empty; Milli had taken Vivi out with Rena for the day to give me a break. I pulled my phone out, just looking at his number sitting there. I became nervous. You can do this,

Divine; just call the man. Why else would he have given you his number if he didn't want you to use it? I pressed call. He answered, but at first, he didn't say anything.

"Hello," I said, thinking I had made a mistake, "maybe he put the wrong number in my phone."

"Divine," he called out, causing me to smile.

"Mr. Ivanov."

"You can call me Gavriil, your Gavriil."

I began shaking my head, "well, Gavriil, my Gavriil. Could I possibly have some of your time today?"

"I wouldn't wish to spend my time any other way."

"Good, then just text me the location, and I'll be there."

Pulling up to the hotel, I looked around before getting out. The place was super fancy. I opened my car door, and some guy was standing there.

"Can I help you?" I asked with an attitude.

"I'll just need your keys so I can park your vehicle."

I smiled, embarrassed. I handed him my keys then quickly walked into the hotel. There was a restaurant in the back. This was where Gavriil told me to meet him. Walking through the beautiful place, I started having second thoughts. I felt like I didn't belong. Turning around, I began walking towards the exit.

"Divine," I heard my name being called.

I looked back, and it was the guy that whispered in Gavriil's ear at the club.

"How do I know you?" I asked suspiciously.

"Hello beautiful, my name is Viktor. I work with Gavriil. Should I escort you to him?"

I was almost to the door.

"I guess I've been caught," I said, smiling.

"Yes, you have," he smiled back.

Taking a seat in front of Gavriil, I couldn't help but wonder. How did he look so damn good every time, like why was his face created so perfectly?

"You tried to run?"

I playfully glared at Viktor, "snitch. I wasn't trying to run. This place makes me uncomfortable," I said honestly.

"Why?" he asked curiously.

"Everyone's staring at me."

"Should I have them clear the place out?" he asked.

I stared at him, trying to see if he was serious. I really felt uncomfortable, plus I wanted to see if he would actually do it.

"Sure," I said, narrowing my eyes at him.

Come on, big man, show me you can clear this shit out. Gavriil lifted his hand, Viktor walked away, and in a matter of minutes, the whole dining area was clear. There was only the waiter, Gavriil and me.

"I wasn't serious, Gavriil," I said, shocked that there were no longer people around us.

"Never say something to me that you don't mean. Whatever you wish for, I will make happen always," he spoke as he looked me in my eyes.

It was at that moment that I realized I needed to be careful with him. Gavriil took me seriously, and I couldn't be reckless with my words or the way I treated him. So, I decided to be honest with him about everything. There was no point in putting on a show.

"Gavriil, would you like to fuck me?"

Gavriil looked at me confused and intrigued, "I thought I would have to put more work in, gain your trust."

"None of that is necessary. I'm a married woman, so I don't want or need those things. I love my husband very, very much. The only thing that I want from you is sex. I'm sure this could be an ideal situation for you, right?"

"An Ideal situation, you say?"

"Yes, I don't want anything from you. And I'm not giving you anything. There will be no commitment between us, just sex."

"Just sex?" he said, repeating my word.

"Yes, Gavriil, just sex. If I call, you answer. If you call, I'll answer. Woo will be aware of our newfound situation. My husband comes first for me in all things. If you feel you don't wish to continue, we can stop. Now, are we going to do this or not?"

Gavriil wiped his brow. He looked away from me, smiling. It was almost as if he couldn't believe the words I had just said.

"And here I thought we would just be having lunch," he stood from his seat, walking over to me. He put his hand out, and I took it, standing. "If this is how you wish for me to have you, then this is how I will have you."

"Great," I said, kissing his lips.

That was the beginning. Who knew that that kiss would seal my fate with the psycho. Now I'm locked in a damn bedroom like a prisoner. My phone vibrates; I have a text from Raylo.

"The twins made it home safe."

Luckily, Woo kept his word. Now I need everything else to go as planned. Then I'll figure out a way to get away from crazy. Do I want to get away? Divine, do not start. What happens to the new us, the free us? Gavriil would try to lock me away; he's already doing it. I can't deal with another man controlling my life, not when I've tasted freedom. I can't fall down another rabbit hole. I love too hard, and I'm tired of my love not being returned.

The Moment

Opening my eyes, I sit up on the unfamiliar bed. I begin looking around the unfamiliar room. How I ended up here begins coming back to me. I'm in Gavriil's house, locked in an annoyingly beautiful room. Gavriil strives for perfection in everything, which is why I'll never understand his dealings with me, the imperfect me. I pull my knees up to my chin then I look out of the window. Why is the sun shining so brightly? I feel like today is going to be an exhausting day.

I stand off from the bed, stretching, and grab my phone. I text the group chat, letting them know I'm still alive after being snatched. I walk into the bathroom; I take a look at myself in the mirror. Why am I smiling? Why am I not pissed? He's holding me hostage. There are things I need to do. Why did he show up last night? Years, it's been years since I've seen him, talked to him, touched him. So why did it feel like time hadn't passed between us last night?

Why did I fit so perfectly in his arms? Why did I want to be in them? Divine, we can't do this, not again. I turn the shower on; I need to relax. Gavriil says I hurt him; how? I never promised him anything besides sex. I was always honest with him. Telling him exactly what I think when I think it, comes easy. There haven't been any secrets between us. I repeatedly told him not to expect anything from me. So how did I hurt him? Stepping into the hot water, I can't keep my mind off all these questions.

Did he wait for me all this time? Does it matter if he did? Am I ready to have that conversation with him? What do I want from him? I feel my heartbeat through my chest with this question. What do I want from Gavriil? Do I want anything? *Sex*, I only used to ever want sex from him. That's not true, and I know it. I slam my fist against the wall. This is frustrating.

I can't understand why he's acting like this. He's Gavriil Ivanov. He's a man that could never get used to hearing no from anyone. So why is he acting so invested in me? Why did he look so hurt after I told him that I thought everything he's said to me were just pretty words? Why did I still cling to them so much? Stepping out of the shower, I grab a towel wrapping it around myself.

I begin looking through the sink drawers; I must be in a guest bedroom. The drawers are filled with toiletries that are wrapped in plastic. So meticulous, I grab a new toothbrush and a comb. Parting my hair down the middle, I begin combing it in sections. I put my wet hair in two cornrows, and then I brush my teeth. Walking out of the bathroom, I see that my bag has been placed on the bed. I look in the corner of the room, seeing a small table filled with food.

Taking a deep breath, I walk over to my bag, taking out my phone charger. I plug it in by the nightstand. Next, I dial Milli's number placing the call on speaker as I begin getting dressed.

"Hello."

"Prisoner number 1 checking in," I say sarcastically.

"Ma, this isn't the time to be joking. Should I come get you?"

"No, Milli, I'm fine."

"Gucci's due date is near."

"I'm aware. I just have to talk to the psycho." I say the last part loudly.

"Did you take care of your things?" he asks, trying to change the subject.

"Yes," I answer.

I don't want him to know what's happened, I may hate Woo, but I don't want Milli hating him.

"I talked to pop last night."

I don't say anything; I don't care.

"He said you put a gun to his head."

I begin shaking my head, "don't worry, Milli, I will not shoot your father again."

"That's not the point. Do you still want to be with him, ma?"

I scrunch my face up, "where is this coming from?"

I hear him take a deep breath, "nothing, never mind."

Fully dressed, I walk over to the phone.

"Take care of Gucci. I'll call you later." I hang up.

What was that about? I walk over to the little table, taking a seat. I begin eating the breakfast that has been laid out for me. What is this man thinking? What am I thinking? Why am I so comfortable with this situation? Seeing him is doing to me exactly what I thought it would do. I like him, I always have. I could never continuously sleep with someone

I didn't like; the problem was that I was devoted to Woo. I'm no longer devoted to him, so now what?

Once I finish eating, I begin staring at the door. I know what Gavriil wants from me, but do I want to give it? I stand walking to the door; I turn the knob, and just like I thought, it opens. I walk out and see Viktor standing against the wall, texting on his phone.

"Why am I not surprised?"

"Because you're used to it," Viktor says, smiling at me.

"Take me to him. Let's get this over with."

"Of course," Viktor says, leading the way.

Following Viktor, I can't help but admire everything. Whoever designed this place thought of everything down to the last detail.

"Whoever did this house for him has amazing taste," I say to Viktor.

"Whoever she says." I can hear the smile on his face.

"Are you trying to tell me Gavriil did all this?"

"Gavriil is a fucking control freak. I thought you knew this?"

"He even does tedious things like this. You would think he'd be too busy."

Viktor stops walking; he turns, facing me. "You would think so. So how does he always find time for you?"

"That's a million-dollar question right there."

Shaking his head, he continues walking. We arrive at huge double doors; Viktor opens the doors for me then walks away. Walking into the room, I see right away that it's an office. Gavriil is standing next to his window on his phone. His eyes find mine. I walk over to a chair sitting in front of his desk and take a seat. I will wait my turn. Gavriil's speaking in Russian; he hasn't taken his eyes off me as I stare back at him. I watch as his lips move, forming sounds; I don't know, I want to kiss them. Divine, re-fucking-lax.

Hanging his phone up, he goes to take a seat in his throne-like chair.

"So were you able to clear your head, do some thinking?" he asks.

"I'm always thinking, Gavriil. These wheels are always spinning."

He doesn't say anything; he sits at his desk staring at me. I believed myself to be a woman that loved attention. I love walking into a room and having all eyes on me. I bask in it because I remember there was a time I would cower away; I would hide behind Woo's back. Today's Divine would never cower, so why am I feeling so exposed as he looks at me? It's like he knows everything there is to know; there's no need for me to speak. However, I wouldn't be me if I let this silence continue.

"Gavriil, why are you being childish? Let me go; I need to get back," I say as confidently as I can.

"Childish," he leans back in his chair, still staring.

"Gavriil," I say, huffing and puffing.

"Little girl."

"Yes, compared to the great Gavriil Ivanov, I'm an immature little girl, so why am I still here?"

"You know why you're still here."

"Look, old man..."

"Old man," he says, cutting me off.

Why does he continue to repeat after me?

"Yes, old man. You are like a thousand years older than me. So go out there and find someone else to play with. I don't want to be here. I'm trying to go about this politely; I have accepted your hospitality. Thank you for breakfast. I will start killing people if you do not let me walk out of here."

I want to leave; I don't want to give myself any room to fall. The only thing that can be heard is my loud breathing.

My adrenaline is high as hell after my little rant. Him looking at me with those beautiful blue eyes isn't helping my excitement.

"I'm only seven years older than you."

I can't help it; I don't want to, but I can't help it. I burst out with laughter, why is he this way?

"Gavriil," I whine out.

He stands walking around his desk until he's standing in front of me. I refuse to look up at him because I know that's what he wants. I also can't look straight ahead because of his dick print. I just close my eyes; I'm trying to have some self-control.

"It's time to get serious, sweetheart," he says, "look at me, Divine."

I slowly lift my head up, looking at him.

"I get it you're afraid, and you should be. After not seeing you for so long, I'm going to be unloading all these feelings you left me with. I'm going to be unloading them on to you. The ridiculous obstacle that once stood in my way has removed itself. That's why you're afraid, right?"

I continue looking into his eyes. I refuse to say anything. Like I said, I'm weak for this man.

"Before, how I felt about you was my problem. My feelings were things that I had to take care of on my own. But after being neglected, abandoned without so much as a goodbye. I think it's your turn."

"What are you talking about?" I ask, confused.

"It's time for you to take responsibility, Divine."

"Responsibility for what?"

Gavriil roughly pulls me out of my seat and into his arms. Taking my hand, he places it on his heart. Just like mine, it's beating fast and hard; the only thing is you'd never be able to tell. Gavriil's poker face shows no emotion. It took years for me to see things in his eye's, but even then, you can't be sure. I look up at him with questioning eyes. He smiles, looking down at me.

"You have to take responsibility for all the wanting, needing, and enduring I've been doing all these years. It has taken everything I have in me to not tie you to my bed. Since I heard you say hello, my body has been in a continuous fight with my mind. I would never do anything to purposely hurt you, but I want you tied to me tightly."

The look in his eyes makes me fidget in his arms. I feel like I'm suffocating. I try to pull away a bit, but he just pulls me closer.

"Your absence has helped me become the heartless lunatic my business needs me to be. But right now, your presence is forcing my closed, broken heart to open again." Poetic as always, only now I don't believe them to be just pretty words.

"At first, you will resist me, fight me, fight yourself. I expect all of that; I can take it. But eventually, inevitably, you will come to me," he kisses my forehead, "and I will open my arms in acceptance because I've been waiting. So go ahead, Divine, keep lying to yourself. Keep trying to lie to me. The longer you take, the harder you're going to fall. I know you a lot better than you think."

I close my eyes. Gavriil's heartbeat has been going insane under my hand. He's saying I'm the cause as if we were teenagers and not adults. He's saying that me being around him is driving him crazy. I feel my eyes water; I shouldn't have come. I should have listened to Milli. Gavriil is trying to hold me captive, and I'm on the verge of letting him. No one has ever said anything like this to me before. It's almost as if words like these are being wasted on me.

Looking into his eyes, I almost get lost in them.

"I can't understand where all of this is coming from." I look away from him, "it was just supposed to be sex."

"For whom? If I remember correctly, and I do, I never agreed to just sex with you. I said that if this is how you wish for me to have you, then that is how I will have you. The time for that has come and gone. Now I will have you the way I want you."

I'm scared to ask; I'm scared of what he will say next. I can't be locked away in a room. That much I do know.

"Gucci's eight months pregnant."

"I'm aware. Go ahead, go to them." He lets me go. "This will be the last time I let you go."

I step away from him, making my way toward the door. I badly want to jump him right now; I want him to fuck me on his desk. But I have to take this chance if he's letting me go. His words have done their job, I believe him. They have moved me till tears are in my eyes. Just as I'm about to make it to the door, one falls.

"Divine," he calls out, "don't try to run or hide from me because one way or another, I am going to find you."

I reach for the doorknob. I'm under attack; my soul is under attack. Fuck it, I've been a fool for much worse. I turn from the door and walk right over to Gavriil, pulling him down to my level.

"Pretty fucking words," I say before kissing him like my life depends on it.

Wrapping his arms around my waist, he lifts me up; my legs instantly go around his. To hell with everything for this moment. A moment I've missed for a long time. Gavriil sweeps everything off his desk. He gently lays me down on it. He begins unzipping his pants. Just from the look in his eyes, I can tell he understands what I want right now, what I need.

No words need to be said. I don't want foreplay. Right now, at this moment, I want to be as close as I possibly can. I want to feel that addicting sensation I used to feel whenever he was inside me. So I pull my panties off. With his pants and underwear down on his ankles, he begins kissing me intensely again. Our bodies have always been compatible; without having to think, my hands just know where to go. Our lips caress each other as our tongues dance. There's no fight; we are both equal. I've always loved kissing Gavriil. He never seeks power; he's never trying to dominate me.

Pulling my hips closer to him, he finds my entrance. We both stop breathing as the feeling we once enjoyed repeatedly comes back to our bodies. Like riding a bike, just because it's been years doesn't mean you've forgotten how to ride. My body is melting right into Gavriil as if it's known him every day. I remember saying I'd never leave this feeling, but then I left it. A fool, I was such a fucking fool.

Thrusting his hips into mine repeatedly, and with the sounds that leave my mouth, the grunts that leave his, this bliss-filled feeling that I stupidly wanted to run from, without my permission, my body begins reaching its peak. I pull Gavriil closer, kissing him deeply. Everything in me wants to be released, but I try to hold on to this feeling for as long as I can; with fingers digging deep into his back, he continues. This makes everything more intensified; I can't take it, I try pulling myself up.

Gavriil, noticing what I'm doing, pins my hands above my head. He stares deeply into my eyes. Still never stopping his rhythm, the look he's giving me is telling me I better not run. Closing my eyes, he begins biting me everywhere, my neck, down my chest, even my cheeks. This will be the first time he's ever left marks on my skin; the thought makes me even more excited; I begin tightening around him. The grunt that comes from his lips makes me smile.

"Ty dlyamenyavse," he begins whispering this to me repeatedly.

This is another first; Gavriil has never spoken to me in Russian while we had sex. All these years and we can still experience many firsts. I force myself to stop thinking. I want to focus on the many sensations Gavriil is putting my body through. I want to enjoy the moment. For once, I don't want to think of the past or the future. I just want to be right here, in these orgasms.

New Life

The ringing of my stupid phone forces me out of my peaceful sleep. It's been so long since I've been in my own bed, that I might just shoot whoever's calling. Grabbing the phone, I swipe it. Unfortunately, it's too bright for me to look at it right now. I don't even have the strength to say hello; I just hold the phone up to my ear. Who the fuck is it?

"Ma," it's Milli, I groan, "Gucci's in labor, and she's asking for you."

I sit right up. After Gavriil and I fucked all over his office, he kept his word and let me come back home. Milli was at the airport waiting for me. I'd literally only been gone for two days; they are spoiled. Just like Gavriil, they refused to let me leave them, so I'd spent the last couple of weeks basically living with them, having to take care of two grownups.

I didn't mind it; I love my babies. I don't mind babying Gucci. She's aware that once the baby comes, all my love will go to him. I've told them both to enjoy me while they can. Anywho, Gucci's hormones have been getting the best of her, plus she is ready to push her baby out. I've been there before, so I understand.

Yesterday Gucci and I got into a big fight; I almost shot her ass. Milli basically put me out, saying maybe we should spend some time apart because of our hormones. That's right, he said 'our,' so I asked him what the hell he was talking about. He looked me in my face and said I needed some dick; I almost committed double homicide. So, I left, came home, took a nice long bath, then got into my perfect bed.

I get up out of my bed with the phone still to my ear. Gucci calls for Milli, and I can hear her in the background crying for me.

"I'm getting dressed now. Are you guys at the hospital?"

"We are pulling in now. I already woke the damn doctor up."

"Okay, tell Gucci I'm on my way."

"Ma," Milli calls out before I can hang up.

"Milli."

"I was on the phone with pop when her water broke. He said he on his way as well."

I take a deep breath, "do you want him here?"

"Yes," he answers quietly. "I would like the both of you to be here for this."

"Alright, I'm on my way."

I don't think anything else of it. If Milli wants Woo here, then that's the way it will be. I didn't raise Milli by myself, and I know how much Woo means to him, even if he is a selfish asshole. After brushing my teeth and throwing some water on my face, I grab my purse and head out of the door. Locking my door, I look at my guard, smiling.

"The baby's coming," I feel excited.

"What are the odds? You leave for one day," Igor says, escorting me towards the elevators.

"That's what I'm saying. I missed my bed," I say, cheesing hard.

I now have two bodyguards that follow me everywhere. One word—Gavriil. He didn't just let me come home; there were conditions, Igor and Sacha. Damn bastard.

"Gavriil, I don't know if you're aware, but I've been living my life for a long time now. I know how to protect myself."

"Divine, it has always bothered me how you walk around alone, conduct business alone. Since you stubbornly insist I stay here, for my peace of mind, I need them to go with you."

I look over at Igor and Sacha; they haven't said a word. They're just waiting for me to lose this argument so they can go pack.

"Igor doesn't even like me."

Gavriil walks over to his mini bar and pours himself a drink.

"That's not true, Divine. Everyone likes you. That's the main reason I want to lock you up."

Oh lord, I'm beginning to get scared; he might change his mind.

"Fine," I stand, "let's go, boys."

"Divine," Gavriil calls out; I sit back down. "You two go pack." They walk out of the office.

I look at Gavriil innocently.

"Don't give me that look. While you're gone, answer all my calls and texts. If you miss just one, I'm coming to get you." He tosses his drink back. I say nothing; he's acting insane. "Divine, do your best to do as I say, enjoy your children and congratulate Million on my behalf. Because the next time I see you, I will not be letting you go."

I nod my head up and down. He launches the glass he was drinking out of at the wall. I take that as my queue, so I stand pouting. I walk over to him, kissing him gently; he grabs me, pulling me closer. His hands move down my back to my ass. He grips it tightly.

"You better go," he kisses my lips, "before I change my fucking mind."

I kiss his lips, letting him go. I don't say anything else; I don't know what to say. I need time to think, get my thoughts in order. Sometime apart should do the trick. If I stay near him longer, I'm going to just do as he says.

Igor opens the car door for me, and I get in.

"Where's Sacha?"

"I called him; he'll be meeting us there." I shake my head ok.

Having them around isn't as annoying as I thought it would be. Igor and I joke about the time I threatened to kill him for trying to frisk me all those years ago. I even got them to tell me stories about Gavriil. Some of them make me feel guilty; they blame me for him being a lunatic. How could that possibly be my fault? Gavriil was born into a mafia family; he was raised to be a killer. He was a damn lunatic way before I came into the picture.

Pulling into the hospital, I jump out of the car. I'm sure I look a mess; I threw on a jogging suit and pulled my hair back into a ponytail. I did bring some hair and makeup things for Gucci. Her ass was adamant about looking like a beauty queen when her son arrived. I tried explaining to her that how she looked would be the last thing on her mind. I still brought them just in case though.

"I'm here for Carver," I say to a nurse sitting behind a desk.

She begins typing away on her computer.

"That floor is a private floor."

"Yes, I'm the one that paid for it to be private. What do you need, my id, my bank account so you can see the transaction?"

I hear a commotion happening behind me, somehow some way, the paparazzi found out about her labor. I'm going to have to clean the house. Somebody is feeding these parasites information.

"Your id, please," she says, looking stupid.

Doing my best to not lash out at her, I hand her my id. She then escorts us up to the fourth floor. I paid this damn hospital a lot of fucking money, Gucci will have the comfort she needs, and Milli will have the privacy he wants. As soon as the elevator doors open, I hear her screams.

"Milli, where is she? I can't push until she gets here."

"She'll be here. Try to stay calm for me, baby," he says, wiping the sweat off her head.

" I'm here," I say, rushing into her room.

I drop my bag and walk to her, grabbing her hand.

"I'm here."

Gucci begins crying, "I'm so sorry, Divine, please don't be mad at me."

I caress her face, "I'm not mad at you, Gucci."

Still sobbing, "Pineapple just tastes really good on pizza."

Holding back my curse words, "we can talk about that later. Let's focus on meeting the young king."

That's fucking right. The huge fight we had yesterday was about some damn pizza. Pineapple just does not go on pizza.

"Ok," she says, nodding her head.

The doctor walks in. She sanitizes her hands then puts her gloves on. She walks over to Gucci and checks her cervix.

"Alright, family, it's time to push," she says excitedly. "Dad, you grab this leg; grandma, how about you grab the other?"

"Divine, I'm scared," Gucci says with tears in her eyes.

"Of what?"

"I don't know." She closes her eyes.

"Hey, look at me." She opens them.

"Don't you see Milli and me standing here? Nothing will happen. Everything is going to be fine. Your precious baby will be in your hands in no time."

"Ok, Gucci, give a big push," the doctor says.

Gucci's whole face turns red as she pushes as hard as she can. I hold back my laughter as I watch Milli's eyes go wide.

"You can do this. Come on, Gucci," Milli says gently.

"Come on, push," the doctor says.

Gucci begins pushing again. "Ok, I see the head; keep pushing."

"I can't," Gucci looks at me. "Please, I just want to go to sleep. I'm tired, please."

"No, baby, we almost at the finish line. Our prize is waiting for us. Don't give up; you got this," Milli says, kissing her hand.

I guess that's just what she needed to hear because she pushes this time long and hard. The doctor pulls the baby out.

Milli begins kissing Gucci all over her snot and tear-filled face.

"You did it, thank you, I love you," Milli whispers,

It's official I hate them both. They are too stinking cute. I can't help the smile on my face as I watch the nurse clean the new little life.

"What are you guys going to name him?" I ask.

"Devin Billion Carver," Milli says, proud.

"Devin is so boring," Gucci says tiredly.

"Well, you shouldn't have made the deal then. If it's a boy, I name him. If it's a girl, you name her. Besides, somebody around here needs to have a normal name."

"Milli, you are annoying. I thought hard while naming you," I say, rolling my eyes.

The nurse takes baby Devin over to Gucci; she places him on her bare chest. I feel my eyes water; I'm so happy right now. I'm so happy I could share in this moment with them.

"He's so handsome," I say, looking at them.

"Ma, he came from me. What you thought?"

Gucci and the nurse begin laughing. I could smack him.

"Where's her bag?" I ask Milli.

"Oh shit," he says, rubbing his head, "I left it."

"It's ok. I'll go get it. I'll bring you a change of clothes too," I say, pointing to the splash of afterbirth on his shirt. I grab my purse walking out of the room.

I say thank you to Alicia, a young maid; she helped me pack Gucci and Milli some things. I told them fools to have this stuff taken care of last week. I walk into the new nursery and grab the one bag they did have ready, Devin's. I make my way out to the car, where both Sacha and Igor stand. They come to me, taking the bags. We load them into the car and head back to the hospital.

"He's the smallest, cutest thing ever," I say as Igor drives.

"Did you hold him?" Sacha asks.

I look out of the window, "I'm not sure I'm mentally ready for that. Holding another baby in my arms."

The car ride becomes quiet. I take a deep breath as we pull into the hospital's parking lot. Stepping out of the car, Igor and Sacha grab the bags, and I try to sike myself out, rid myself of any negative thoughts; today is a happy day. If I don't fix my face, I know Milli will start hounding me. Walking into the hospital, I see Milli's guards have cleared the lobby—it seems he's got control over the situation now. I smile at them, getting on the elevator.

Once the elevator doors open to their floor, I can feel a bad vibe. I step off and look to the left in the waiting area. There sits Asia and Bobby; there are a couple of unfamiliar guards standing around them. Even if I wanted to, I can't hide the disgust shown on my face. Bobby has a little girl lying in her lap, the nerve.

Asia looks up at me, "Oh my god," she stands, walking over to me. She gives me a hug that I don't return, "you still look fucking gorgeous. How are you, how have you been? Believe it or not, I've missed your mean ass." She is going a mile a minute; she still hasn't changed.

"Thank you, and I'm fine," I look behind me, "you guys can take the bags in there." Igor and Sacha walk into the room.

"I thought Gucci said she didn't want anybody in there," Asia says.

"I'm sure that just applied to you two," I answer truthfully.

"Still evil," she says.

I find myself staring at Bobby and the little girl. I thought if I ever saw the two of them that I'd pull my gun out, shooting them. Yet here I stand, and there they sit, and I feel nothing, fascinating. I guess it's true what they say. Time cures all. Well, I guess that works in everyone's case except Gavriil's. My phone begins vibrating; I pull it out, looking at it. Why did I even think of him?

I answer, walking away from Asia, "Hey."

"Divine," he says.

I already know what he's calling about. Igor and Sacha walk out of the room laughing. This is going to be a long day. I glare at them, who snitched? They look at me, and Sacha quickly points at Igor.

"Milli told me he was on the phone with him when Gucci's water broke," I begin explaining before he can even ask. I need him to relax. "Milli says he wants him here, and you know I can't tell him no." I'm getting a headache.

"I hear his wife and child are there," Gavriil says.

My eyes go straight to Bobby's. Like the rest of the room, she's watching me. I look down at her left hand, and sure enough, there is a fucking ring. Now that hurts a bit. He married her and was all over me like a month ago. She follows my eyes and looks down at her ring; she covers her hand. This is why I hate her ass. She's always running from her bullshit, stand tall in it, hoe.

"They are here," I turn my back to them.

"I take it you didn't know?"

"Of course, I didn't know Gavi. I don't keep up with that man."

" Are you ok?" It's just a question, but it makes me smile. Why does he always care?

"Yes, I'm fine. I'm shockingly fine," I answer. It's hard to get used to this.

"And the baby?" Gavriil asks. I glare at the snitches again, and this time Igor points to Sacha.

"You have them report everything to you?"

"Yes, I'd kill them otherwise. Don't change the subject."

"I don't know. I guess I'm scared that I'll go to a negative place. I don't want to bring the mood down; you know today isn't about me."

"Shall I come get you,"

"Gavriil," I whine out.

"Well, you threatened my men and me if I didn't let you go. Now you're afraid that you'll have your buried memories come back just from holding the baby."

"I just don't want to be depressed," I say lowly.

"Well, that's too bad, love; your experience was a horrible one. It's ok to be depressed. I'd wonder about your sanity if you weren't. Go hold your grandchild."

"Don't say it like that," I begin laughing.

"You give me shit for being seven years older than you, and you're somebody's grandma." I begin laughing harder. "Go be with your family. I'm being called away."

"Ok." He hangs up.

Things feel different with Gavriil. He's always asking me if I'm alright, always wondering how I feel. Besides having two shadows that lurk behind me 24/7, this is one of the harder things to get used to. Walking into Gucci's hospital room, I see Woo sitting on the couch holding Devin. He looks up at me, smiling. I nod my head acknowledging him, then walk over to the bags.

"Asia says you won't allow anyone in," I ask Gucci.

"Fuck them, hoes. I don't want them around my baby." Looks like tough Gucci is back.

"Come on, let's get you showered," I begin helping her out of bed.

"Take your shirt off," Woo says to Milli.

"Why?" Milli asks, taking his shirt off.

"That skin-to-skin contact shit," Woo answers.

"I thought only Gucci did that."

"You his father, right?"

"Yes," Milli says with attitude.

"Then shut the fuck up. Come here before he falls asleep again."

Milli walks over to Woo, taking a seat beside him. Woo places the baby in his hands.

"Support his head," Woo says to Milli.

I smile, walking into the bathroom with Gucci.

"I still don't like his ass," I hear her whisper.

She sits on the toilet as I turn the shower on. I walk out of the bathroom, grabbing Gucci's things out of her bag. I grab the makeup and hair supplies I brought. Now that I know them hoes are here, I can't have my baby girl out of here trashed. Once she's dressed and her hair is laid, she comes out; I had the nurse change her sheets and clean her suite.

"Ok, Milli, your turn," I say, handing him his bag.

He walks Devin over to Gucci and then takes his bag from me.

"Try to see if he'll latch on," I say to Gucci.

"He's sleep."

"Trust me, he'll smell that milk," I say, laughing.

I give her a little blanket so she can cover herself.

"When you finish feeding him, let them come see the baby. I'm sure that child out there is hungry." I glance at Woo's dumbass.

"Them dudes that walked in here with you are Russian, right?" Woo asks, ignoring my comment.

"Don't start," I say, placing a pillow under Gucci's arm so she can be comfortable.

"I just asked you a question, Divine. Those Gavriil's men?"

Closing my eyes, I take a deep breath, "yes, Woo."

"You back sleeping with the enemy?"

"Who's enemy?" I walk over to the window.

"Divine, don't play with me. You know what the fuck I mean."

"No, Woo, I'm sorry I don't. Don't fucking worry about me. You need to be worried about that little girl that's been sitting out there this whole time. Or what about your wife? Don't sit here and question me, then think I owe you answers because I fucking don't."

I turn away, trying to calm down.

"Ma," I hear Milli call out, "did you bring my lotion?"

I go into Gucci's bag, grabbing hers, then I walk it over to him.

"So, you with Gavriil now?"

I stare at him, none of these people around me take me seriously.

"I don't know," I answer truthfully. "We are in a weird space."

Woo stares at me, rubbing his beard, "when did this weird space happen?"

"The day I needed the acid."

Woo sits back, getting comfortable on the couch. Gucci is on the bed cursing about the pain Devin is putting her nipples in. Milli walks out of the bathroom. The room is tense.

"What happen?" Milli asks Gucci.

"Woo asked about Igor and Sacha," she says.

"Pop," Milli calls out, "no drama, remember?"

"I remember," Woo says, standing and walking out.

Milli follows him out. I go take a seat on the couch. I put my head back, closing my eyes.

"I'm sleepy," Gucci says

I stand grabbing Devin from her; I place him in the little bed next to hers.

"Eat something first."

"Later, please," she whines out.

I help her get under the covers, "ok, but you need to eat properly in order to produce his milk."

"Ok, grandma," she says, closing her eyes. I should smack her.

Milli walks back in, "he went to check them into a hotel."

"He should have done that in the first place. Did you know they got married?" Milli looks away from me, "is that why you were so worried about me still wanting him?"

"I just want you happy," I smile.

"Milli, I'm in charge of my own happiness. I'll be fine."

My phone begins vibrating; I have a call.

"Hello."

"Boss lady, I feel neglected," Raylo says.

"I have a lot going on. What's up?"

"Nothing, I was checking in."

"The only thing in my life that I don't have to worry about," I say to myself.

"An old friend of ours has popped back up."

This gets my attention, "who?"

"Korky."

Just hearing his name pisses me off, yet another thing Woo left unfinished. I basically spent my time and resources cleaning up after him.

"I got it. We'll talk about this later. Leave it be for now."

"You got it. Tell Million congratulations for me." I hang up.

"Everything good, ma?" Milli asks.

"Yeah, everything's good. Have you set a date for when you are dropping the album?"

"Well, now that she's had the baby, I'm thinking of dropping it next month."

I walk over to him then pull him into a hug. I hold him tightly; it's never mattered that I'm only eight years older than him. That when Woo and I took him, we were just children too. I taught him how to read, how to write, how to tie his shoes, how put his clothes on properly. I took care of him as if he was a child Woo and I brought into the world. I had to grow up so fast, so young. It's been so long since I just hugged him.

On the outside, looking in, you wouldn't believe that I was his mother. You wouldn't understand why he holds Woo and me so close to his heart, why he had to do and learn so many horrible things before he turned eighteen. Or why his young mother had a change of heart, why she pulled him so far away from the life he was raised to live. I've always believed him to be better than us; he is.

I pull away from him with tears in my eyes. I look over at a sleeping Gucci.

"Are you happy?" I ask.

"I'm a simple man, ma," he says, standing tall. I begin laughing, "as long as you and her smile. I got everything I need." We both turn towards Devin; he's moving around.

I pick him up, holding him in my arms. Then just like that, they fall, the tears I'd been holding on to fall. I stare at his precious little face; my little baby will have the world. I'm sure Milli is prepared to take care of this little new life. I also know that I now have to be prepared to live mine.

Future Sealed

It's been two weeks since Gucci had the baby, and Devin has been kicking their ass. I sit back in the rocking chair with Devin. I can't help remembering how Vivi had Woo and me up all night. If you ask me, Milli and Gucci have it easy; they have me. I've been living with them, helping them get used to being parents. Right now, the two of them are passed out in the house somewhere tired.

"That's right, baby, you keep them on their toes," I say to Devin.

His big eyes are wide open. I smile down at him as he begins sucking his lips, feeding time.

Walking out into the hallway, "locate Gucci," I say to one of the guards.

He begins talking into his earpiece. I wait patiently.

"She's in her bedroom, mam."

"Thank you," I say, making my way down the hall.

Walking into their bedroom, I see Milli passed out on the bed. I hear the shower running. I walk back out into the hall.

"Have someone bring some food up here," I say to a different guard.

Walking back into the bedroom, I no longer hear the shower. I take a seat at the table in the corner of the room. Gucci walks out in a towel; she looks over at me smiling, then she heads into the closet. Once she's dressed, she wakes Milli up. Without a fight, he gets up heading into the bathroom to shower as well.

"He's hungry," I say, looking down at Devin.

Gucci takes him from me. She has a seat across from me and begins feeding him.

"I don't think I'll ever get used to this here bullshit," she says, referring to the pain.

"You will," I say, pulling my phone out.

I have 3 missed calls. There's a knock at the door; I stand going to open it. Two maids walk in with a cart full of food. They take it over to the table and begin setting it. Gucci smiles at them, thanking them. I stand at the door, still looking at my phone. If I don't answer him, I know he's going to fucking flip. But I don't know how to respond to his request.

"More time. Plzzzzz."

I text.

The maids leave out. I close the door and walk back over to the table. I take a seat, sighing. Milli walks out of the bathroom and into the closet.

"What's wrong, Divine?" Gucci asks.

I scrunch my face up at her, "Divine?"

"Ma," she says, correcting herself.

"Better and nothing."

"Why you keep looking at your phone like you stressed?" she says, looking right at me.

I narrow my eyes at her; she just smiles. This heifer knows what she's doing. Milli walks out of the closet. He comes taking a seat next to me.

"Ma, what's wrong?"

"Nothing, Milli, I'm fine."

"Her boyfriend probably wants her to come home," Gucci says, smiling.

"He's not my boyfriend, and this is my home."

My phone begins vibrating. It's Gavriil; I look at Gucci. Somehow this is her fault. I don't know how but since she's being aggravating, I'm blaming her.

"Hey," I answer the phone.

"No," he says sternly.

"Why?" I whine back.

"It's time for you to come back. We have many things we need to discuss."

"So, after we talk, I can come back?"

"Divine, do I need to come get you?"

I don't say anything. I begin staring at a painting they have on the wall.

"I guess you don't think I'll come. Just sit tight. I'm on my way."

"No, I know you'll come."

"Then why the games, Divine?"

"I'm not playing games."

"Then I'll be seeing your beautiful face tomorrow night for dinner. Yes?"

I roll my eyes, "fine."

"Very good," then he hangs up.

I smack my lips, putting my phone down on the table. I feel myself smiling. I look at Gucci, and she has that stupid smile on her face. I look over at Milli, and he's staring at me, shocked.

"What?" I say, irritated.

"I told you, baby. She acts like a child whenever she talks to him," Gucci says to Milli.

"Ma," Milli looks closer at me, "are you blushing?"

Instinctively my hands fly to my face. "No, it's just a bit warm in here."

I begin eating.

"Are you leaving?" Milli asks, eating his food. Gucci stands then goes to lay Devin down in his bassinet.

"You know she is. If she doesn't, he's going to come snatch her again." I'm happy she finds my situation amusing.

Ignoring her, I look at Milli, "Why, do you want me to stay?"

"At first, I did, but after watching your face light up, I think you love that white man."

I begin pouting, "no, Milli, you're supposed to tell me not to go."

"Ma, gone on ahead back to your boyfriend and don't think I don't know you ignored what I said."

"Your mafia boyfriend," Gucci adds.

I sit back in my chair, ignoring them both. I fold my arms, huffing. I do not act like a child when it comes to Gavriil. Now I have to get on a plane and fly back to him. Would he really come to get me if I refused? Divine, you know the answer to that.

"I've changed my mind. I'm going back home," I say as I step off the jet Gavriil sent for me.

Igor and Sacha both begin laughing. There are four cars waiting for us. Viktor is standing next to one of them.

"This is a bit much," I say, walking up to Viktor.

"You should tell him that when you see him," Viktor says, smiling as he opens the door for me.

"You should tell him that when you see him," I mock, getting into the car while rolling my eyes.

As I look out of the window, I realize that I have no idea where I'm being taken. Nothing we drive by looks familiar. I sigh, sitting back; it's not like I have control over the situation. I close my eyes, letting them rest for a bit. I'm tired and need my rest for the war that's about to begin. I have no idea what Gavriil is going to say to me.

"Divine, Divine, Divine," I hear my name being sung. The sound is pulling me out of my sleep.

"I'm awake," I open my eyes.

I'm still in the back seat of the car, and Viktor is looking at me through the rearview mirror. I grab my mirror out of my purse and look myself over. Once I've deemed myself presentable, I look back at Viktor.

Stepping out of the car, he opens my door, "you snore."

I smile innocently. He leads me into what looks like a fancy restaurant.

"Oh, Vicky, it's so good to see you," the hostess says giving Vik a kiss on his cheek.

Her attention moves to me. She looks me up and down, taking in all of me. Everything about me screams perfection, from the diamonds on my wrist to the weave gracefully laid on my head. My face is perfectly painted, my eyebrows are laid. The heels that I stand in are high, and the maroon dress I wear hugs me tight. So, somebody tell me, why this hoe has her face scrunched up as she looks at me? I begin smiling my million-dollar smile; this makes her scoff.

"Watch it," Viktor says warningly.

The little blowup doll fixes her face immediately. She turns, leading us to our table. I follow behind Viktor as two guards I don't know follow behind me. As we walk through the packed restaurant, all eyes turn towards me. There was a time when I would feel uncomfortable, even small. However, Gavriil has brought me to enough of these bougie places that the looks I get no longer faze me. In fact, I keep a bright smile on my face, looking down at them as I walk past. It must suck for the men to know that they can't have me and the women to dream that they were me. That's right, bitches, hate yourselves while wishing you were me.

Blow up doll stops at a door, opening it for Viktor. He steps to the side, letting me walk in. I can't help the now genuine smile on my face as I see Gavriil standing by the window yelling at someone on the phone. He looks at me; I watch as his eyes scan my entire body. Obviously, this turns me on. I walk over to him, wrapping my arms around his broad shoulders and kissing his dreamy lips.

"I've actually missed you," I say, smiling.

He hangs up on whoever he was yelling at.

"Me calling and texting you every day wasn't enough?" he asks sarcastically.

I shake my head.

"Come sit, let's feed you."

He pulls a chair out for me; I take a seat. Blond dumb hoe walks in, Viktor closes the door behind her.

"What can I get for you this evening, Mr. Ivanov?"

I tune out their conversation. I'm sure Gavriil is going to order for me anyway. I text the chat, letting them know I landed safely and that I fell asleep in the car, which's why I didn't text back sooner. I mute the conversation, then put my phone down. I begin smiling at whatever her name is. I'm sure my dazzling smile is making her uncomfortable.

"Will that be all, sir?" she asks, looking at Gavriil nervously.

He doesn't say anything else to her. He begins staring at me. I stare back at him; we enter our own little world.

"So, what did you get me?"

"It's a surprise. How is your grandchild?"

I roll my eyes playfully, "he's wonderful, so tiny," I say, cheerful.

"I'm glad you're in a good mood. I'm also happy you decided to come to me on your own."

"I don't like being dragged around," I say while scrunching my face up.

"It's time for us to finish having that serious conversation."

A new waiter walks into the room. He pours wine into both of our glasses; I don't take my eyes off Gavriil. Once he's filled them, he walks back out.

"Shall we begin discussing how you'll be spending the rest of your life?"

"Gavriil," I say worriedly, "the rest of my life?"

"Divine, I told you when you left that that would be the last time I let you go. Now I don't know if you've forgotten, but I am and always have been a man of my word. Why do you doubt the things I say to you?"

"It's not that I doubt them; they just don't make any sense. I can't understand you."

"You shouldn't try to. I don't make logical decisions when it comes to you."

"See, that is what I mean. You say things like that, and I don't know how to take them. For years you and I have had an arrangement where we tried to not make things personal."

"You tried," he says, cutting me off.

"Alright, I tried. All we did was have sex. We'd sometimes eat, then have sex. There was never anything extra that would have pointed us into this direction."

"What direction?"

"The direction where you kidnap me. Pursue me relentlessly."

"Divine, I have always pursued you, maybe not relentlessly, but I have been pursuing you."

"Then what changed?"

"You left. Since we started this 'arrangement,' I have had a very likable interest in you. The more time we spent with each other, that interest grew. And as it grew, I began expressing this to you. The fact that you chose to ignore and not believe me is not my problem. Every time you came to me, you were in pain. That is why I treated you delicately, gently." He picks his glass up, taking a sip. "I realize that in the beginning, you weren't really comfortable sleeping with me, yet it was your idea. And as time went by, you became attached. You becoming attached to me little by little is what gave me hope while sustaining my desires."

"Then you disappeared; I couldn't hear your voice or see your face. Divine, what you need to understand is that while you were coming to me little by little, I was already enslaved by your existence. You had already had me, I was already yours to use as you wished, and you did."

"Gavriil," I say, trying to slow this conversation down a bit.

"I'm not finished," he says, causing me to close my mouth. "Today will be the last time we discuss if how I feel is real or not."

The door opens, and the waiter walks in with our food. This time I'm looking away from Gavriil; I'm too scared. I feel like a child being chastised. The waiter leaves, and I become nervous; I look at him again so he can continue.

"Your love for Woo also helped with keeping me at bay. As I began understanding you more and more, I realized there would be no way for me to come in between you two. I realized that if I was serious and truly wanted you, that I would have to wait for your relationship with him to implode. I have always taken everything you've said to me seriously. I believe everything you've ever told me, except the things you say when it comes to me, your body speaks for you." He begins eating his food, and I look down at mine.

"That fucker did a number on you, warped your whole way of life. I've told you the way you guys loved is not the only way."

"Are there better ways?" I ask, looking up at him.

"Of course, Divine, the world is much bigger than the one he tried to keep you locked up in. Now eat."

I pick my fork up and begin eating. Everything in my head is scrambled; this food is delicious though. I'm going to have to learn the name of this dish. I look up as Gavriil puts two small boxes on the table in front of me. I place my fork down then I wipe my face with the napkin.

"Divine, I'm going to ask for a lot from you. Things between you and I will become different."

He opens one of the boxes; it's a ring that matches the one he wears on his right hand, the ring that represents his family.

"Why do things have to become different? Why can't they remain as they are? We can stay right here; nothing has to change." I am becoming anxious.

"Everything is going to change. Right now, you are seen as nothing to me. That's unacceptable. You are something; you are everything. I will be taking all of you from now on. I will finally have you the way I want to have you."

"I don't know if I'll ever be able to give all of myself to someone again," I say honestly.

I don't ever want to be hurt or betrayed. My eyes begin watering; the fuck is going on. I am not weak.

"You can, and you will. That devotion that you once wasted, I'll have it."

"What about you? Is Gavriil Ivanov going to give himself to me? Would your family or the world even allow you to?"

Why does he ignore the huge elephant in the room? We are different in more ways than one. Gavriil sits back in his chair, narrowing his eyes at me. I look away because I don't understand what he's looking for. I always feel like he's seeing right through me.

"Fuck," I hear him say under his breath, "is that what all this has been about?"

"What are you talking about?" I ask, confused.

"You have been sitting your beautiful ass across from me, sleeping with me all these years thinking you're not good enough for me?" He begins talking in Russian.

"That's not it. I just know that whenever you and I walk anywhere together, I get dirty looks. I might not know everything, but I do know that your Bratva is very family-oriented. I'm sure that my beauty won't matter, but my skin tone will. You've only pulled me into your world a little, and I can clearly see that I'm not welcomed."

"Those fucking wheels always spinning. I'm the fucking boss," he says, frustrated.

"Gavriil." He slams his fist on the table, cutting me off.

"Shut the fuck up, Divine," his accent is thick, "Do I look like a man that can be told what to do, who to love?"

"Love?" I say, shocked that the word left his mouth.

"Have I not been speaking English? What do I need to do for you to comprehend what I'm trying to convey to you?"

I begin staring at my wine glass. He's saying he's in love with me out loud. Those words are being put into the air.

"Stop that," he says; my eyes shift to his, "stop fucking thinking. It seems that's been the fucking problem this whole damn time."

"You love me?" I ask pathetically.

Before answering my question, he opens the other box. Inside there's a huge diamond ring.

"These are both yours. Though I want to, I can't put them on for you. I am becoming impatient. Put the rings on. Accept that I love you and that I will have you. You will become Divine Ivanov, or I can just take you back to my house and keep you locked up for the rest of your life. I am fine with either choice."

I look down at the boxes in front of me. I know he's serious; he will lock me up in that damn house. A second marriage though?

"I'll still be able to run and take care of my business?"

"If you choose to wear my rings, you will have all the freedom you want. If you choose not to, my home is all you will see."

How did I manage to attract this psychopath? How did I manage to like this psycho? I grab the diamond ring looking at it.

"The moment you put that on your finger, it will become our engagement ring."

"Shouldn't you be down on one knee putting this on my finger?" I don't look up from the ring; I'm too nervous to look at him right now.

"Under different circumstances, yes, that would be the case. However, this is you I'm dealing with. I want you to choose. I need for you to choose."

Some choices. I slide the ring on my finger. I hold my hand out, admiring the ring. Why does he know my ring size?

"What if I don't want that one?" I say, pointing to his family ring.

"They come together," he answers, sipping his wine.

I grab the ring looking at it. Why do I feel like putting this on will be too much work?

"Beautiful, listen to what I have to say before you put that one on," he says.

I pause, looking at him. He stands, walking over to me; he pushes my chair back so that he can kneel in between my legs. Where was this energy with the engagement ring?

"This is an agreement that will be written in blood. In the end, there will only be death to separate us. I will not be sharing you, nor myself. For the rest of your life, there will only be me. You already have all of me, but with this ring, you will be gaining much more. Never take it off and never go back on the promise of belonging only to me." Gavriil smiles, "Breathe."

I let out the breath I didn't know I was holding.

"I will not forgive, even if it's you, Divine. Never go back on the promise. Everything that is mine will become yours. That is what we will mean once you have both rings on your fingers."

Gavriil makes sure he looks deep into my eyes; he wants me to take this seriously. I slide the ring onto my finger, smiling brightly. Gavriil takes both my hands in his; he lifts them up one at a time, kissing them. I've just sealed my fate to a man that I'm sure is crazy, that I'm sure loves me. It's been a long time since I was sure about being loved.

Korkscrewed!

"Divine, don't you think it's a bit early?" Igor says from the driver's seat.

I don't answer. He's right; it's too fucking early. I'm surprised I found the strength to get dressed. I look at my phone; it's seven am. I look out of the window as we drive through the middle-class neighborhood. The homes are beautiful. We pull over in front of the nicest house on the block. Since I left so early, I was able to sneak off with just two other cars following me. If Gavriil had it his way, I'd be ten cars deep.

Sacha gets out of the car, making his way over to my side. He opens the door for me.

"Did you call first?" Sacha asks.

Ignoring him as well, I step out of the car, yawning. Six guards stand around watching everything. I walk up the walkway, pulling out my spare key. The house is simply decorated, much like him. I make my way up to his bedroom, and I walk in. There, Raylo is lying peacefully, with some random girl beside him. I take a seat in a chair he has in the corner of his room. Igor and Sacha stand at the door, shaking their heads.

I pull my phone out as I glare at his sleeping figure. I dial his number, wondering where his phone is—it better be stolen. His phone's ringtone breaks through the silence of the room. I watch as he reaches over without looking at it, sending whoever is calling him to voice mail. I close my eyes taking a deep breath, then dial his number again. It rings again.

"Just answer it," the nameless girl smartly says, half asleep.

"Yes, why not just fucking answer it?" I say, letting my presence known.

Raylo jumps up, turning towards me with a surprised look on his face. He has his pistol in hand. I look at my phone then back at him.

"Ten, that is the number of times I have called you."

"Boss lady, what's up?" he says, rubbing his face.

"You," I say, pointing to the girl, "get the fuck out."

She stands with the sheet still wrapped around her. She grabs her things then rushes past Igor and Sacha.

"You," this time I'm pointing at Raylo, "get up, get showered and meet me in your kitchen."

I stand, making my way out of his bedroom and down to the kitchen. I'm in need of some caffeine. Walking into the kitchen, I realize Raylo's simple ass only has a coffee pot. As much money as he's making, he can get a fucking Keurig. I begin making a pot. I open his refrigerator, I pray he has some good creamer; I may kill him if he doesn't. My eyes land on a French vanilla creamer. I smile, pulling it out. I begin looking through his cabinets for mugs.

"You boys want coffee?" I ask my shadows.

Igor shakes his head.

"I'll have a cup," Sacha answers.

I pull three cups out and wait for the pot to finish.

"Boss is awake," Igor says, looking down at his phone.

Like magic, my phone begins ringing.

"Good morning," I say, cheerfully.

"Where are you?" His voice sounds rough.

"Someone woke up on the wrong side of the bed?" I say, grabbing the pot.

"Divine."

"I'm at Raylo's, and from here, I'll be going to one of my warehouses,"

"You should have woken me up. I don't like waking up alone."

I begin pouring the coffee into the mugs, "if I had woken you up, you would have kept me in bed."

"That's where I like you best."

I smile, "of course it is. I have to take care of this. Because of you, I've been putting it off."

"Fine," he begins talking in Russian to his background.

"Cream?" I ask; Sacha shakes his head.

I scrunch my face up.

"I'll text you. Someone's at our door," Gavriil says, sounding irritated.

"Bye," I say as he hangs up.

Gavriil has bad phone etiquette. That's probably why we used to text so much. Raylo walks into the kitchen, picking up his mug.

"Invasion of privacy."

"You should have answered your damn phone."

"Well, it was my night off; I needed to relax. Give me my key back."

I pout, "no, it's mine."

I look out at the scenery as we pass by buildings and trees.

"I see you've got a new leash around your neck," Raylo says, motioning towards my engagement ring.

I smile, looking down at it, "it's a tight one too, and yet it couldn't possibly be as tight as this one," I put my right hand out for him to see.

"That's deep."

"Too deep; I still don't understand his obsession." Both Igor and Sacha begin shaking their heads. "What? I'm just saying Gavriil Ivanov is a big fucking deal, and I'm not saying that I'm small time. I would just think he'd be more into the innocent, young virgin type."

They start speaking to each other in Russian. I block them out, not caring. I'm sure they're just going to snitch anyway.

"Raylo, how long do you think it will take for them to get Korky?"

"I'm not sure. If you would have put me on it, you know I would have had him hanging upside down from the ceiling yesterday."

"Which is why I didn't put you on it. You are not a worker anymore. You're the boss. You can't get your hands dirty as you did before. Now let the younger ones do it. How will they learn if we keep doing every damn thing?"

"I don't need to be out here getting comfortable. Putting in work keeps my eyes open, keeps me wired."

"I'm happy I got you in the divorce," I say, smiling.

"Shit, who wants Slim? He and Woo were meant for each other."

We pull up to the warehouse, and I look around, noticing things are different.

"You like what I've done?" Raylo says, proud. I nod my head, still looking around. "I got security everywhere. I got shit like we are a real company. Everybody don't have access to everything like before, and best of all, I created the new security system."

"I told you, you should have just taken that scholarship you were offered."

Raylo could have been like the next Bill Gates or some shit. He was always into technology, but like most of us, the need to survive trumped all.

"I'm cool. Besides, there wasn't shit they could teach me that I couldn't teach myself."

"If I knew you wouldn't be killed for it, I would kiss you right now."

"No, thanks, I don't want those kinds of problems," he laughs, stepping out of the car.

Walking through the warehouse, I can't believe my eyes. Everything is so organized and clean; this shit looks like a legit ass business, you know, without the guns and drugs all over the place. This is the first time I've been in here. Before I relocated, I bought a couple of properties and told Raylo to do as he saw fit. At the time, I really wanted to get away, but I would never leave Raylo high and dry. Sure, The Village is enough for me, but I knew he had a vision. One of the best decisions Woo ever made was making Raylo come with me that day to go pick Milli up from school.

That day we talked and laughed the whole way there and back. We became good friends. As we became bigger, it was clear whose side he'd choose to be on. Woo had everyone else. All I had was Raylo; he's always been more than enough. Like me, he doesn't like confrontation, but he'll meet that shit head-on. We like things to be neat and solved quickly, which is why we work so well together.

"Raylo, this shit is perfect. After seeing the Village, I knew leaving things to you was perfect."

"I do what I can. You leaving everything to me let me know how you trusted me. You know me, Divine; I don't want or need much. I like surviving and maintaining."

"I still don't know how I feel about that. Be power-hungry a little bit more," I say, laughing.

"For what?" he looks around the warehouse, "in this game, the leaders are the ones that usually go first."

"You must be delusional," he looks at me confused, "you are the damn leader; I'm what they call a benefactor. Show me your office."

Walking into the office, I have a seat at the desk.

"Maybe we should have gotten breakfast first," Raylo says, sitting across from me.

"Business first, food later. Now how long do you think they're going to take?"

"I gave them all the info they needed. They promised results by today."

"When did you put them on it?" I ask, curious.

"Right after you text me," Raylo says, texting on his phone.

"That was the day before yesterday. Maybe I should have just gone."

Raylo looks up at me from his phone.

"What?" I say, annoyed.

"From how early you pulled up on me, it looks like yo ass snuck out. How you gone be out here kidnapping somebody when you got to sneak out?"

"Fuck off."

Before I can finish telling Raylo about himself, there's a knock at the door.

"Come in," Raylo says loudly.

The girl that was in his bed just a couple of hours ago walks in. I smile, looking at her now; she's dressed in men's clothes. She even carries herself as a man would. Thinking about it reminds me of Bobby. I look away.

"Liv," she glares at him, "I mean Ace, this is Divine; Divine, this is Ace."

Looks like she already has her claws in him.

"Nice to see you, in clothes," I say, smiling.

She begins blushing innocently. Then she clears her throat getting into her mean demeanor. Yep, this is another Bobby.

"The guys are here," she says, looking at Raylo, then she leaves back out of the office.

"Mixing business with pleasure," I say, standing.

Raylo shrugs, "she's cute."

"If you like it, I love it." We walk out of the office and downstairs to my prize.

Raylo grabs a chair, placing it in the middle of the room. Many men and women stand around waiting for the show that's about to be put on. I take a seat, thanking Raylo. A black van backs into the warehouse. Raylo motions for his men to open the door and bring out our guest. Korky is dragged out of the back of the truck, and as I requested, his knees have been bashed in. They drag him to the middle of the room, laying him on the floor in front of me. I honestly don't like violence; I hate torture, but I despise snitches.

Korky looks around the room bewildered. I'm sure he has no idea why he's here, nor does he know these people. You see, after Korky fulfilled his snitch job with the feds, they sent him away. Only a fool would have returned, and here the fool was. He didn't know that Milli and Raylo saw him that day. No one messed with him or said a thing. He thought he could just come home and get back to business.

After looking around the room, his eyes finally find mine. I look down at him, disgusted.

"Divine," he says, shocked.

"The one and only," I say, dryly.

"What's going on? Where's Woo?"

I look over at Raylo, laughing; Raylo shakes his head.

"Korky, you've been a nasty boy."

A look of confusion crosses his face. I speak before he can start lying.

"How many people have you given to the feds?" His eyes grow big. "What, you thought nobody knew? Sure, years have gone by, and many others may have forgotten. But not Divine, no, I remember."

"Look, I didn't give them nothing on you or Woo. I was stuck. I had to give them something, but I never gave them yall."

"You seem to be mistaken about many things. Woo can take care of himself; he is also none of my concern. I can also take care of me just fine." I stand walking over to him; I kick his body over so that he's now on his back. I place the heel of my shoe in his chest.

"Now stop wasting my fucking time. What did you give the feds?"

"Divine, I swear on my son, I didn't give them anything on you. I may have given them some information on some of your young boys."

I push my heel into his chest, "Like who?"

He doesn't say anything, which basically confirms my suspicions. I lift my foot and walk back over to my chair, taking a seat. This is yet another mess I have to clean up. Raylo signals one of his guards; the guard walks over to Korky with a sledgehammer, slamming it into his right hand. The sound that leaves Korky makes me cringe.

"Korky, you are going to die today, whether you give me what I want or not." I pause for dramatic effect. "I've never liked you, so you being a snitch didn't come as a surprise. However, you almost got someone very important to me locked up. I know that Woo told you Milli and Raylo would be the ones making the drop that day."

His eyes move over to Raylo, who's still on his phone.

"So here are your choices..."

"Choices," he says, cutting me off.

Before I can say anything more, Raylo has somehow quickly made it over to Korky, kicking him in the face. Korky spits out some blood, and I think I see teeth as well; I look at Raylo, smiling. He doesn't look at me as he continues whatever he was doing on his phone.

"Korky, I promise I will give you a chance to speak. Don't cut me off. Now, as I was saying, here are your choices. It is a fact that you will die here today; however, you don't have to die alone. Let's say, for instance, your girlfriend and son, or what about the young girl you have pregnant now? All these innocent, oblivious people can die with you. Or you can just tell me what they have on Milli and only you die."

I look at Korky as he breaks down into tears. He was once a man that stood tall, someone who believed he could do whatever he wanted. Now here he is lying on the floor, his blood surrounding him, crying like a sad child.

"Fuck you, Divine!" he shouts.

"Very well," I say, pulling my phone out.

"Wait," he shouts, causing me to freeze, "they don't have anything on him because they could never find the bodies. That's why they let me go."

I look at Raylo; he has a big smile on his face.

"Shit happens for a reason, boss lady," Raylo says, shrugging his shoulders.

"Shut it, Ray." I look around the room; I don't recognize a face around here. My phone begins vibrating; it's Gavriil. "He's all yours," I say, turning away.

"Hey," I answer.

"Love, have you eaten?" I smile.

"No, not yet."

I hear Korky scream painfully loud.

"How about lunch?" Gavriil asks.

"Sure, I'm outside already." I begin hearing screams coming through the phone. What the hell is he up to?

"Gavriil?"

"Yes, love."

"Where are you?"

"I'm at home. I told you we had a guest."

I roll my eyes; he's a damn psychopath. "Just text me where you want to meet. I'm just about finished here."

Gavriil's background quiets down.

"Well, what do you know? I'm just about finished here as well."

"Bye," I say, hanging up first.

Gavriil is a complete psycho.

Igor and Sacha escort me into Gavriil's favorite restaurant. Blonde blow-up doll is at the hostess podium again. I'm not in the mood to be nice, so I glare at her. She does the best she can to avoid eye contact. I begin shaking my head, it must be my ring. Ever since I put it on, people don't even look me in the eye. All the shady and unwelcoming stares I used to get seem like some distant dream I was having. I find it amusing. Igor does the talking, and I follow as she shows us to our private room.

I walk in and begin smiling.

"So, you're my lunch partner?"

"Gavriil's hands got tied a bit tighter, and he didn't want you to be alone," Viktor says, smiling.

"Well, I find your company comforting." Sacha pulls my chair out for me; I thank him, taking a seat. "What have you guys been up to?" I ask, smiling at the nervous blow-up doll; she hands Vik the menu and quickly bolts out. I giggle at her expense.

"Nothing much, same as you, I suppose," he leans back a bit.

I know I shouldn't, but I can't help thinking about it and now that I have him alone, why not?

"So, Vik, my guy," he looks at me with his brows raised, "why is Gavriil going through all this?"

"All what, Divine?"

"All this," I say, putting both my hands up. "You don't think it's weird he's trying to let in an outsider?"

"Trying? Outsider?" he says, smiling.

"Yes, I'm an outsider. Don't you guys have like codes and traditions?"

"We do, but all those things flew out of the window the moment he saw you."

I think back, "you mean after that gunfight when I looked a bloody mess with a pregnant belly?"

"Oh Divine," he says, shaking his head, "Gavriil knew of your existence before he ever saw you in person."

I look at Viktor, confused; he chuckles.

"Black came to Gavriil before he started working with you and your ex-husband. Gavriil, needing to know all, sent me to take pictures and learn information on the new kids. I must say watching you two come up has been inspiring. The first time Gavriil saw you was in picture form. You were in a baby store all alone shopping for clothes." These fucking creeps. "Watching him look at your picture every day after that, I realized he was too far gone. So, you see, Divine, outsider or not, your fate was sealed long before you knew it."

I smack my lips, looking away from him. He just made me feel stupid, and what's up with Gavriil falling for a pregnant married woman? I feel embarrassed. I won't question it anymore; I'll go with the flow. This man truly loves me. I hear the door open, pulling me out of my thoughts. Viktor stands, buttoning his suit jacket. Before I can turn to see him, Gavriil's hand wraps around my shoulder, pulling my chin towards him; he gently kisses my lips.

"I have missed you," he says, looking at me.

I smile, "we slept in the same bed last night."

"But you left me."

"I had to."

"Don't do it again."

I pull my face from his hand, "ok."

He walks over to the seat that Viktor was just sitting in. Gavriil begins speaking, but I don't hear a word he says. I'm so focused on his lips as they move, imagining the different places I want them to kiss. His ridiculously sharp jawline, covered in smooth, soft hair. Fuck, I want to run my fingers through his beard. My lips part as I release the breath I was holding. Gavriil tilts his head, narrowing his eyes at me. My eyes move to his; a slow smirk appears on his face. He raises his hand, telling whoever was at the door to leave. I hear the door open and shut. My eyes have not left Gavriil's face. Why is he so fucking attractive?

"If I didn't know any better, I'd say my Divine is hungry for something other than food."

I begin smiling. Without saying a word, I stand, making my way over to his side of the table. Pushing back in his chair, he allows me to straddle him. I run my fingers through his beard, caressing his jawline. He closes his eyes, welcoming my touch. I begin attacking his lips; this lust came out of nowhere. Gavriil's hands make their way to my ass, squeezing tight; I moan out a bit as he kisses me down my neck. Why are his lips always so fucking soft? I begin unbuckling his belt. I hear him chuckle.

I don't find anything funny; I have an itch that I need his dick to scratch. It doesn't take much; he was already standing tall, waiting to be unrestrained. I feel my mouth begin to water as I look at how hard he is. I hear Gavriil chuckle again. This time I glare at him. I'm sure I look crazy; shit, I am crazy. How could I not be? This man wants to give me everything, and I want to take it all. Gavriil puts both his hands behind his head, leaning back. Is this a challenge? I bite my lip as I position myself over Gavriil perfectly. I reach down, moving my thong to the side, before slowly moving down.

I begin rotating my hips slowly; I'm scared that if I go any faster, I'll become undone. We are still out in public. Why do I feel invincible when I'm with him? I can do anything. I never have to concentrate too hard; Gavriil's dick is always hitting my spot no matter the position. It's like his dick was created just for me. I feel his hands move to my hips; my slow movements must be getting to him; now he sees how I always used to feel. He changes my rhythm to a faster one, and I give in. My hands find the back of his chair for balance. I toss my head back as I feel his lips all over my chest.

Gavriil wraps his arms around my waist tightly, then stands. He pushes everything off the table then lays me down on it. I giggle at him. Now he's the one that looks crazy. He pulls out of me, causing me to pout.

Pulling on my thong, "you don't need these," he rips them off.

Gavriil then pulls me up, turning me towards the table and bending me over it. He slaps my ass hard, causing all my nerves to jump in excitement. I feel him enter me once again. He's so violent that I can't keep up. Sorry to this table that others may eat on, I'm about to cum all over it. His roughness ignites something even more in me. How could our bodies just go so well together? There's a knock on the door; this startles me.

"Keep squeezing me like that, see if I don't fuck you right here for hours," Gavriil says as he continues. He's ignoring the door, and I'm nervous that someone might walk in.

I want him to stop, but I feel so good. I can't help the sounds leaving my lips; I also can't help the water in my eyes. I try reaching behind me, pushing his legs back. He just holds my arms on the table. I try standing; he just puts his upper body over mine. I'm stuck in the endless pleasure, and I'm excited because someone may walk in and see me. I know I look fucked up right now. Gavriil is fucking me so hard that I feel the table moving beneath me. I begin feeling it, that unforgettable feeling in the pit of my stomach. That wonderful feeling that I've fallen in love with.

Everything begins shaking; it's uncontrollable. No matter how hard I try to contain it, I become undone. My knees become weak, I can no longer hold myself up. Gavriil grabs me as he finishes as well. He stands me up as my back hits his bare chest. Where did his dress shirt go? He pulls my dress down for me then pulls the chair up for me to sit lazily in. I watch as he puts his undershirt back on over his sweat then his dress shirt. Here I am looking a thoroughly fucked mess, and he looks like he's headed to work.

Gavriil walks to the door; he opens it, talking to whoever's out there. I feel the exhaustion coming on. Maybe I should have slept in. He walks back over to me, helping me up.

"What about the food?" I ask as my stomach growls.

"We'll get it to go. We have a flight to catch."

Gavriil wraps his suit jacket around me.

"A flight?" I ask, confused.

He begins laughing as he lifts me into his arms.

"Yes, love, I told you we are going to my home country."

"Russia? When did you tell me we were going to Russia?" I ask, leaning my head on his shoulder.

"When you were looking at me like you wanted to eat my lips off."

I smile, closing my eyes. I'm tired. I woke up way too early this morning, then Gavriil took all the energy I had left. I begin falling asleep. The happiness I feel right now can't be compared to anything I've ever felt before. The only thing that could make me feel even better is if Vivi were here with me. I know that's impossible. I look forward to my future with Gavriil. Though I didn't want to, I find myself hoping again.

Russia, here I come!

To be continued…

Still to Come

Coming April 2022

The Streets Divine Book II

Coming May 2022

The Streets Divine: Roberta's Regret

www.ingramcontent.com/pod-product-compliance
Lightning Source LLC
Chambersburg PA
CBHW020218260626
47156CB00002B/443